Ed Langley and his crew of space scientists had spent four years in space. Their mission had been to develop the super-drive of their ship, and to gather information about other stars and planets. They had also 'gathered' an alien with some remarkable powers, Saris Hronna, who had asked to go with them to Earth. But the superdrive had caused some unforeseen problems. Instantaneous transfer through hyper-space did weird things to time. When they reached Earth, it was six thousand years older than when they left – and a lot of changes had been made . . .

'Poul Anderson is one of the very finest science fiction authors around. THE LONG WAY HOME is a tight, smooth, dazzling novel of the far future. There's a malignant race of non-human telepaths, secret hideouts in the Hima-layas, decadent latter-day Roman-type orgies, and lots of other good stuff packed away in this solid, exciting novel'
Inside Science Fiction

Also by Poul Anderson in Panther Books

Poul Anderson

The Long Way Home

Panther

Granada Publishing Limited
First published in Great Britain in 1975 by
Panther Books Ltd
Frogmore, St Albans, Herts AL2 2NF

To Hallie Kruse with thanks

CHAPTER ONE

THE spaceship flashed out of superdrive and hung in a darkness that blazed with stars. For a moment there was silence, then:

'Where's the sun?'

Edward Langley swiveled his pilot's chair around. It was very still in the cabin, only the whisper of ventilators had voice, and he heard his heart thutter with an unnatural loudness. Sweat prickled his ribs, the air was hot.

'I . . . don't know,' he said finally. The words fell hard and empty. There were screens on the control panel which gave him a view of the whole sky, he saw Andromeda and the Southern Cross and the great sprawl of Orion, but nowhere in that crystal black was the dazzle he had expected.

Weightlessness was like an endless falling.

'We're in the general region, all right,' he went on after a minute. 'The constellations are the same, more or less. But—' His tones faded out.

Four pairs of eyes searched the screens with hunger. Finally Matsumoto spoke. 'Over here . . . in Leo . . . brightest star visible. Do you see it?'

They stared at the brilliant yellow spark. 'It's got the right color, I think,' said Blaustein. 'But it's an awful long ways off.'

After another pause he grunted impatiently and leaned over in his seat toward the spectroscope. He focused it carefully on the star, slipped in a plate of the solar spectrum, and punched a button on the comparison unit. No red light flashed.

'The same, right down to the Fraunhofer lines,' he declared. 'Same intensity of each line to within a few quanta. That's either Sol or his twin brother.'

'But how far off?' whispered Matsumoto.

Blaustein tuned in the photoelectric analyzer, read the answer off a dial, and whipped a slide rule through his fingers. 'About a third of a light-year,' he said. 'Not too far.'

'Much too far,' grunted Matsumoto. 'We should'a come out within one A.U. on the nose. Don't tell me the engine's gone haywire again.'

'Looks that way, don't it?' murmured Langley. His hands moved toward the controls. 'Shall I try jumping her in close?'

'No,' said Matsumoto. 'If our positioning error is this bad, one more hop may land us right inside the sun.'

'Which'd be almost like landing in hell or Texas,' said Langley. He grinned, though there was an inward sickness at his throat. 'O.K., boys, you might as well go aft and start overhauling that rattletrap. The sooner you find the trouble, the sooner we can get back home.'

They nodded, unbuckled themselves, and swung out of the pilot room. Langley sighed.

'Nothing you or I can do but wait, Saris,' he said.

The Holatan made no answer. He never spoke unnecessarily. His huge sleek-furred body was motionless in the acceleration couch they had jury-rigged for him, but the eyes were watchful. There was a faint odor about him, not unpleasing, a hint of warm sunlit grass within a broad horizon. He seemed out of place in this narrow metal coffin, he belonged under an open sky, near running water.

Langley's thoughts strayed. *A third of a light-year. It's not too much. I'll come back to you, Peggy, if I have to crawl all the way on my belly.*

Setting the ship on automatic, against the unlikely event of a meteor, Langley freed himself from his chair. 'It shouldn't take them too long,' he said. 'They've got it down to a science, dismantling that pile of junk. Meanwhile, care for some chess?'

Saris Hronna and Robert Matsumoto were the *Explorer's* chess fiends, they had spent many hours hunched over the board, and it was a strange thing to watch them: a human whose ancestors had left Japan for America and a creature from a planet a thousand light-years distant, caught in the trap of some ages-dead Persian. More than the gaping emptinesses he had traversed, more than the suns and planets he had seen spinning through darkness and vacuum, it gave Langley a sense of the immensity and omnipotence of time.

'No, t'ank you.' The fangs gleamed white as mouth and throat formed a language they were never meant for. 'I would rather this new and surprissing dewelopment consider.'

Langley shrugged. Even after weeks of association, he had not grown used to the Holatan character – the same beast of prey which had quivered nose to spoor down forest trails, sitting as hours went by with dreamy eyes and a head full of incomprehensible philosophy. But it no longer startled him.

'O.K., son,' he said. 'I'll write up the log, then.' He pushed against the wall with one foot and shot out the doorway and along a narrow hall. At the end, he caught himself by a practiced hand, swung around a post into a tiny room, and hooked his legs to a light chair bolted in front of a desk.

The log lay open, held by the magnetism of its thin iron backstrap. With an idleness that was a fight against his own furious impatience, the man leafed through it.

Title page: United States Department of Astronautics, I/S *Explorer*, experimental voyage begun 25 June 2047. Mission: development of the superdrive; secondary mission: gathering information about other stars and their hypothetical planets.

Crew:

Captain and pilot: Edward Langley, age 32, home address Laramie, Wyoming; graduate of Goddard Academy, rank of captain in the Astronautic Service, spaceman since his late teens. Long record as pilot of exploratory trips, including the Mercury run. Medal of Merit for heroism in *Ares* rescue. (*Hell, somebody had to do it, and if they knew how scared I was at the time—*)

Engineer and electronician: Robert Matsumoto, age 26, home address Honolulu, Hawaii, former space-force marine, present rank A/S lieutenant. Work on Luna, Mars, Venus; inventor of improved fuel injector and oxygen recycler.

Physicist: James Blaustein, age 27, home address Rochester, New York, civilian. Work on Luna for the A.E.C. Politically active. Major contributions to physical theory, creator of several experimental systems for testing same.

Biologist: Thomas Forelli – *Well, Tom is dead. He died on that unknown planet we thought was safe, and nobody knows what he died of – disease, acute allergy, any of a thousand deaths that a billion years of alien evolution could prepare for creatures from Earth. We buried him there, committed his soul to a God who somehow seemed very far away from that green sky and talking red grass, and went on. It's going to be hard to tell his people.*

Langley's eyes raised themselves to the photograph above the desk. The red-haired girl smiled at him across a mist of years and leagues. *Peggy, darling,* he thought, *I'm coming home.*

She would have grown thin, poor kid, and though she said nothing there would be an emptiness of long nights within her, and she would often hold their child – the child he had never seen – close to her. Spacemen had no right to get married. Still less did they have a right to venture beyond the sun, riding a witch's broom of a ship whose engine no one really understood. But when the offer came to Langley,

she had seen the enormous hunger in his eyes and told him
to go. Pregnant and unsure, she had still given him to the
high stars and herself to aloneness.

> '*O wha is this has done this deed,*
> *And tauld the king o' me,*
> *To send us out, at this time of the year,*
> *To sail upon the sea?*'

None but myself, he thought.

Well, this was the last time. He was getting too old for the
work, his strength and speed imperceptibly lessened, and
there was a lot of pay and bonuses saved up. He'd come
home – incredibly, he would be home again! – and they'd
settle down on the ranch and raise pure-bred horses, and at
night he would look up to the wheeling constellations and
smoke his pipe and trade a friendly wink with Arcturus.

His son would not own merely sterile Luna, frigid Mars,
poisonous galling hell-hole of Venus. He would have the
splendor and mystery of a whole galaxy for range, his metal
horses would pasture between the stars.

Langley riffled through the logbook. It was only half a
journal, the rest was page after page of data: engine per-
formance, stellar locations, planetary orbital elements, planetary mass and temperature and atmospheric composition, a
universe grasped in a few scribbled figures. Somehow, the
dryness of it cheered him, brought the chill dark down to a
thing he could handle.

Langley stuffed his pipe with the few remaining shreds in
his tobacco pouch. There was a trick to lighting it and keeping it going in null-gravity. Thank heaven this ship had been
equipped with everything available and a lot unknown
before she was built; most boats, you couldn't smoke at all,

oxygen was too costly. But it had been understood that the *Explorer* would be heading for strange shores. Small though she was, she had the engines and reaction-mass tanks of a cruiser, she could land directly on any planet the size of Earth or less, could maneuver after a fashion in atmosphere, could support her crew for years, could run tests on every imaginable factor of environment. Designing her alone had been a six-year, ten-million-dollar job.

He reflected on the history of space travel. It was not very old. Most engineers had doubted that it would ever become very important. The space stations were useful, the Luna bases had military value, but aside from that the Solar System was a hostile barrenness whose only interest seemed to be scientific knowledge and, possibly, fissionable elements. Then the physics journals had carried an announcement from Paris.

LeFevre was only investigating electron-wave diffraction patterns to test certain aspects of the new unified-field theory. But he had been using a highly original hookup including a gyromagnetic element, and his results – blurred dark rings and splotches on a photographic plate, nothing spectacular at all – were totally unexpected. The only interpretation he could make was that the electron beam had gone from one point to another, instantaneously, without troubling to cross the intervening space.

At California they used the big accelerators to power a massive beam, almost a gram of matter, and confirmed the data. In Kerenskygrad, the theoretician Ivanov had gotten excited and come out with an explanation that fitted the observed facts: the continuum was not four-dimensional, there were no less than eight possible directions at right angles to each other – a modification of the old wave-mechanical hypothesis of one other universe co-existing with ours. The matter had gone through this 'hyperspace'; as far as our universe was concerned, it had gone from point to point instantaneously.

Instantaneously! It meant that the stars and their uncounted planets were a wink away!

Ten years of development, and a shell loaded with instruments leaped from a space station near Earth almost to the orbit of Pluto. When it was found by its radiosonde, the instruments said that no time had been required for the passage, and the animals aboard were unharmed. There was only one trouble – it had emerged a good many millions of miles from the point where it was supposed to. Repeated experiments gave a huge percentage of error in the positioning controls, one which would add up hopelessly and dangerously in crossing light-years.

Ivanov and the engineers agreed that this was merely due to the Heisenberg uncertainty principle, whose effects were grossly magnified by the particular circuits used. It was simply an engineering problem to refine the circuits until a spaceship could be brought out almost exactly where she was wanted.

But such work required plenty of room, lest the error pile up the ship on a planet – or even more disastrously, inside one – and so that the instrument readings would be large enough to permit meaningful assays of the result of making changes in the circuits. The obvious answer was to send a laboratory ship out with a crew of experts, who would make improvements, test them with a long jump, and make still further alterations. The answer was known as the United States Interplanetary Ship *Explorer*.

Langley went through the record of the past year, the erratic leaps from star to star, cursing and sweating in a tangle of wires and tubes, blue flame over soldering irons, meters, slide rules, a slow battle slogging toward victory. One cut-and-try system after another, each a little better, and finally the leap from Holat back toward Earth. It had been the philosophers of Holat whose non-human minds, looking at the problem from an oddly different angle, had suggested the final, vital improvements; and now the

Explorer was coming home to give mankind a universe.

Langley's thoughts wandered again over worlds he had seen, wonder and beauty, grimness and death, always a high pulse of achieving. Then he turned to the last page and unclipped a pen and wrote:

'19 July 2048, hours 1630. Emerged an estimated 0.3 light-year from Sol, error presumably due to some unforeseen complication in the engines. Attempts to correct same now being made. Position—' He swore at his forgetfulness and went back to the pilot room to take readings on the stars.

Blaustein's long thin form jackknifed through the air as he finished; the gaunt sharp face was smeared with oil, and the hair more unkempt even than usual. 'Can't find a thing,' he reported. 'We tested with everything from Wheatstone bridges to computer problems, opened the gyromagnetic cell, nothing looks wrong. Want we should tear down the whole beast?'

Langley considered. 'No,' he said at last. 'Let's try it once more first.'

Matsumoto's compact, stocky frame entered; he grinned around his eternal chewing gum and let out some competent profanity. 'Could be she just got the collywobbles,' he said. 'The more complicated a hookup gets, the more it acts like it had a mind of its own.'

'Yeah,' said Langley. 'A brilliant mind devoted entirely to frustrating its builders.' He had his coordinates now; the ephemeris gave him the position of Earth, and he set up the superdrive controls to bring him there just outside the remaining margin of error. 'Strap in and hang on to your hats, gents.'

There was no sensation as he pulled the main switch. How could there be, with no time involved? But suddenly the spark of Sol was a dull-purple disk as the screen polarized against its glare.

'Whoops!' said Matsumoto. 'Honolulu, here I come!'

There was a coldness along Langley's spine. 'No,' he said.

'Huh?'

'Look at the solar disk. It's not big enough. We should be just about one A.U. from it; actually we're something like one and a third.'

'Well, I'll be—' said Matsumoto.

Blaustein's lips twitched nervously. 'That's not too bad,' he said. 'We could get back on rockets from here.'

'It's not good enough,' said Langley. 'We had ... we thought we had the control down to a point where the error of arrival was less than one per cent. We tested that inside the system of Holat's sun. Why can't we do as well in our own system?'

'I wonder—' Matsumoto's cocky face turned thoughtful. 'Are we approaching asymptotically?'

The idea of creeping through eternity, always getting nearer to Earth and never quite reaching it, was chilling. Langley thrust it off and took up his instruments, trying to locate himself.

They were in the ecliptic plane, and a telescopic sweep along the zodiac quickly identified Jupiter. Then the tables said Mars should be over there and Venus that way—Neither of them were.

After a while, Langley racked his things and looked around with a strained expression. 'The planetary positions aren't right,' he said. 'I think I've spotted Mars ... but it's green.'

'Are you drunk?' asked Blaustein.

'No such luck,' said Langley. 'See for yourself in the 'scope; that's a planetary disk, and from our distance from the sun and its direction, it can only be in Mars' orbit. But it's not red, it's green.'

They sat very still.

'Any ideas, Saris?' asked Blaustein in a small voice.

'I iss rather not say.' The deep voice was carefully expressionless, but the eyes had a glaze which meant thought.

'To hell with it!' Recklessly, Langley sent the ship quartering across her orbit. The sun-disk jumped in the screens.

'Earth!' whispered Blaustein. 'I'd know her anywhere.'

The planet hung blue and shining against night, her moon like a drop of cool gold. Tears stung Langley's eyes.

He bent over his instruments again, getting positions. They were still about half an Astronomical Unit from their goal. It was tempting to forget the engines and blast home on rockets – but that would take a long while, and Peggy was waiting. He set the controls for emergence at five thousand miles' distance.

Jump!

'We're a lot closer,' said Matsumoto, 'but we haven't made it yet.'

For a moment rage at the machine seethed in Langley. He bit it back and took up his instruments. Distance about forty-five thousand miles this time. Another calculation, this one quite finicking to allow for the planet's orbital motion. As the clock reached the moment he had selected, he threw the switch.

We did it!

There she hung, a gigantic shield, belted with clouds, blazoned with continents, a single radiant star where the curving oceans focused sunlight. Langley's fingers shook as he got a radar reading. The error this time was negligible.

Rockets spumed fire, pressing them back into their seats, as he drove the vessel forward. Peggy, Peggy, Peggy, it was a song within him.

Was it a boy or a girl? He remembered as if it were an hour ago, how they had tried to find a name, *they* weren't going to be caught flatfooted when the man brought the birth certificate around. O Peggy! I miss you so much.

They entered the atmosphere, too eager to care about saving fuel with a braking ellipse, backing down on a jet of flame. The ship roared and thundered around them.

Presently they were gliding, on a long spiral which would take them halfway round the world before they landed. There was a dark whistle of cloven air outside.

Langley was too busy piloting to watch the view, but Blaustein, Matsumoto, and even Saris Hronna strained their eyes at the screens. It was the Holatan who spoke first: 'Iss that the much by you talked of city New York?'

'No ... we're over the Near East, I think.' Blaustein looked down to the night-wrapped surface and a twinkling cluster of light. 'Which is it, anyway?'

'Never saw any city in this area big enough to show this high up without a telescope,' said Matsumoto. 'Ankara? There must be unusually clear seeing tonight.'

The minutes ticked by. 'That's the Alps,' said Blaustein. 'See the moonlight on them? Bob, I know damn well there's no town that size *there*!'

'Must be near as big as Chicago—' Matsumoto paused. When he spoke again, it was in a queer, strained tone: 'Jim, did you get a close look at Earth as we came in?'

'More or less. Why?'

'*Huh?* Why ... why—'

'Think back. Did you? We were too excited to notice details, but – I saw North America clear as I see you, and – I should have seen the arctic ice cap, I've seen it a million times from space, only there were just a few dark splotches there – islands, no snow at all—'

Silence. Then Blaustein said thickly: 'Try the radio.'

They crossed Europe and nosed over the Atlantic, still slowing a velocity that made the cabin baking hot. Here and there, over the waste of waters, rose more jewels of light, floating cities where none had ever been.

Matsumoto turned the radio dials slowly. Words jumped

at him, a gabble which made no sense at all. 'What the devil?' he mumbled. 'What language is that?'

'Not European, I can tell you,' said Blaustein. 'Not even Russian, I know enough of that to identify – Oriental?'

'Not Chinese or Japanese. I'll try another band.'

The ship slanted over North America with the sunrise. They saw how the coastline had shrunk. Now and then Langley manipulated gyroscopes and rockets for control. He felt a cold bitterness in his mouth.

The unknown speech crackled on all frequencies. Down below, the land was green, huge rolling tracts of field and forest. Where were the cities and villages and farms, where were the roads, where was the world?

Without landmarks, Langley tried to find the New Mexico spacefield which was his home base. He was still high enough to get a wide general view through drifting clouds, he saw the Mississippi and then, far off, thought he recognized the Platte, and oriented himself mechanically.

A city slid below, it was too remote to see in detail but it was not like any city he had ever known. The New Mexico desert was turned green, seamed with irrigation canals.

'What's happened?' Blaustein said it like a man hit in the stomach. 'What's happened?'

Something entered the field of view, a long black cigar shape, matching their speed with impossible ease. There was no sign of jets or rockets or propellers or – anything. It swooped close, thrice the length of the *Explorer*, and Langley saw flat gun turrets on it.

He thought briefly and wildly of invasions from space, monsters from the stars overrunning and remaking Earth in a single year of horror. Then a brief blue-white explosion that hurt his eyes snapped in front of the ship, and he felt a shiver of concussion.

'They shot across the bows,' he said in a dead voice. 'We'd better land.'

Down below was a sprawling complex of buildings and

open spaces, it seemed to be of concrete. Black fliers
swarmed over it, and there were high walls around. Langley
tilted the *Explorer* and fought her down to the surface.

When he cut the rockets, there was a ringing silence. Then
he unbuckled himself and stood up.

He was a tall man, and as he stood there he gave an impression of grayness, a gray uniform, gray eyes, black hair
prematurely streaked with gray, a long hooknosed face
burned dark by the light of strange suns. And when he
spoke, there was grayness in his tone.

'Come on. We'll have to go out and see what they want.'

CHAPTER TWO

LORD BRANNOCH DHU CROMBAR, Tertiary Admiral of the
Fleet, High Noble of Thor, ambassador of the League of
Alpha Centauri to the Solar Technate, did not look like a
dignitary of any civilized power. He was gigantic, six and a
half feet tall, so wide in the shoulders that he seemed almost
squat; the yellow mane of a Thorian chieftain fell past ears
in which jeweled rings glittered to the massive collarbone,
the eyes were blue and merry under a tangled forest of brow,
the face was blunt and heavy and sun-browned, seamed with
old scars. His lounging pajamas were of Centaurian cut,
complete with trousers, and overly colorful; a diamond loop
circled his throat. He was also known as a sportsman,
hunter, duellist, a mighty lover and a roisterer with an un-
surpassed knowledge of the dives on a dozen planets. The
apartment which his enormous body seemed to fill was over-
crowded with color, ornament, trophies, hardly a book-
spool in sight.

All of which fitted in well enough with his character, but

was likewise maintained as camouflage for one of the shrewdest brains in the known universe.

It might have been observed that the drink in his hand as he relaxed on the balcony was not his home planet's rotgut but one of the better Venusian vintages, and that he sipped it with real appreciation. But there was no one to notice except four monsters in a tank, and they didn't care.

Morning sunlight flooded over him, gilding the airy spires and flexible bridgeways of Lora against a serene heaven. He was, as befitted his rank, high in the upper levels of the city, and its voice drifted to him in a whisper, the remote song of machines that were its heart and brain and nerve and muscle. At only one point in his visual range did the smooth harmony of metal and tinted plastic end, where the city dropped clifflike four thousand feet to the surrounding parks. The few human figures abroad on the flanges and bridgeways were ants, almost invisible at this distance. A service robot rolled past them, bound for some job too complex for a merely human slave.

Brannoch felt relaxed and peaceful. Things were going well. His sources of information were operating quietly and efficiently, already he knew much about Sol which would be of value when the war started; he had bagged a dragon in Minister Tanarac's African preserve, he had won grandly the last time he visited Luna Casino, he had bought a very satisfactory girl a few days ago, the last mail ship from Centauri had reported his estates on Freyja were yielding a bumper crop – of course, the news was more than four years old, but still welcome. Life could be worse.

The apologetic buzz of the robophone interrupted his reflections. Too lazy to get up, he steered the chair over to it. Someone who knew his special and highly unofficial number was calling, but that could be a lot of people. He thumbed the switch, and an unfamiliar face looked at him. The caller bowed ritually, covering his eyes, and said humbly: 'Audience requested with you, my lord.'

'Now?' asked Brannoch.

'P-p-presently, my lord, when c-convenient.' The stutter would be taken for the normal nervousness of an underling in such an august presence, in case this secret line was tapped – which Brannoch knew very well it was. Actually, the pattern of repeated consonants was an identifying pass-word. This was Varis t'u Hayem, a petty Minister and a captain in the Solar militechnic intelligence corps, dressed in civilian clothes and wearing a life-mask. He would not be reporting in person unless it was a matter of urgency. Brannoch led him through a routine of giving his assumed name and business, told him to come up, and cut the circuit. Only then did he allow himself a frown.

Rising, he made a careful check of the concealed robo-guns and of the needler under his own tunic. It *could* be an attempt at assassination, if Chanthavar's counterspies had learned enough. Or it could—

He went swiftly over t'u Hayem's background, and a wry, half-pitying grin twisted his mouth. It was so easy, so terribly easy to break a man.

You met this proud, ambitious aristocrat, whose only real fault was youth and inexperience, at a couple of receptions, drew him out – oh, simple, simple, with the dazzling glow of your own birth and rank behind you. Your agents in his corps got his psychorecord for you, and you decided he was promising material. So you cultivated him, not much, but even a little attention from the agent of a foreign power was overwhelming if you were a High Noble, an admiral, and an ambassador. You pulled one or two wires for him. You introduced him to really top-flight company, gorgeous apparelled nobles of every known state, their magnificent women, their cultivated conversation and splendid homes and rare wines. You gave him the idea that he was listening at the door to plans which would shake the stars— Naturally he did some favors for you, nothing to violate his oath, just stretching a point here and there.

You took him to pleasure houses operated with real imagination. You got him gambling, and at first he won incredible sums. Then you moved in for the kill.

In a few days his fortune was gone, he was sunk a light-year down in debt, his superiors were getting suspicious of him because of his association with you, his creditors (who were your creatures, which he did not know) attached his property and wife – you have him. And for some three years, now, he had been your spy within his own corps, because only you and your organization propped him up, and because even a tiny illegality performed for you made it possible to blackmail him. Some day, if he gave you something really valuable, you might even buy his wife (with whom he was so foolish as to be in love) and give her back to him.

Very easy. Brannoch had neither pleasure nor pain in making a tool out of what had been a man. It was part of his job; in so far as he had any feeling about his broken men, it was one of contempt that they should ever have been so vulnerable.

The outer door of the suite scanned t'u Hayem's fingers and retinae and opened for him. He entered and bowed with the proper formulas. Brannoch did not invite him to sit down. 'Well?' he said.

'Most radiant lord, I have information which may be of interest to you. I thought I had best bring it personally.'

Brannoch waited. The pseudo-face before him twitched with an eagerness that some might have thought pathetic.

'My lord, I am as you know stationed at Mesko Field. The day before yesterday, a strange spaceship entered Earth's atmosphere and was made to land there.' T'u Hayem fumbled in his tunic and brought out a spool which he threaded into a scanner. His hands shook. 'Here is a picture of it.'

The scanner threw a three-dimensional image above the

table top. Brannoch whistled. 'Stormblaze! What kind of a ship is that?'

'Incredibly archaic, my lord. See, they even use rockets – a uranium-fission pile for energy, reaction mass expelled as ions—'

Brannoch enlarged the image and studied it. 'Hm-m-m, yes. Where is it from?'

'I don't know, my lord. We referred the question to the Technon itself – records division – and were told that the design is of the very earliest days of space travel, well before gravity control was discovered. Possibly from one of the oldest of the lost colonies.'

'Hm-m-m. Then the crew must be – have been – outlaws. I can't see explorers taking off knowing they wouldn't be back for perhaps thousands of years. What about the crew?' Brannoch turned a knob, and the next image was of three humans in outlandish gray uniform, clean-shaven, hair cut short in the style of Solar Ministers. 'That all?'

'No, my lord. If that were all, I wouldn't have considered the business so important. But there was a nonhuman with them, a race unknown to anyone including the records division. We got a picture, snapped hastily—'

The alien was shown running. Big beast – eight feet long including the thick tail, bipedal with a forward-crouching gait, two muscular arms ending in four-fingered hands. It could be seen to be male and presumably a mammal, at least it was covered with smooth mahogany fur. The head was lutrine: round, blunt-snouted, ears placed high, whiskers about the mouth and above the long yellow eyes.

'My lord,' said t'u Hayem in a near whisper, 'they emerged and were put under arrest pending investigation. Suddenly the alien made a break for it. He's stronger than a human, trampled down three men in his path, moved faster than you would think. Anaesthetic guns opened up on him – rather, they should have, but they didn't. They didn't go off! I snapped a shot at him with my hand blaster, and the circuit was dead – nothing happened. Several others did too. A small robot shell was fired after him, and crashed. A piloted scoutplane swooped low, but its guns didn't go off, the control circuits went dead, and it crashed too. The nearest gate was closed, but it opened for him as he approached it. One man close by focused a neutral tracker on him as he went into the woods, but it didn't work till he was out of its range.

'Since then, we have been striving to hunt him down, there are patrols all over the district, but no trace has been found. My lord, it doesn't seem possible!'

Brannoch's face might have been carved in dark wood. 'So,' he murmured. His eyes rested on the image of captured motion. 'Quite naked, too. No weapon, no artifact. Are there any estimates of the range of his . . . power?'

'Roughly five hundred yards, my lord. That was approximately the distance within which our apparatus failed. He moved too fast for longer-range weapons to be brought against him in those few seconds.'

'How about the humans?'

'They seemed as shocked as we, my lord. They were unarmed and made no attempt to resist us. Their language was unknown. At present they are under psychostudy, which I imagine will include a course in Solar, and I've no access to them. But the records division tells us, from the documents aboard, that the language is—' T'u Hayem searched his memory. 'Old American. The documents are being translated, but I haven't been told of any findings made.'

Old American! thought Brannoch. *How old is that ship, anyway?* Aloud: 'What other material do you have?'

'Stats of all the documents, pictures and whatever else was found aboard, my lord. It . . . it wasn't easy to get them.'

Brannoch grunted indifferently. 'Is that all?'

T'u Hayem's mouth fell open. 'All, my lord? What else could I do?'

'Much,' said Brannoch curtly. 'Among other things, I

want a complete report on the findings of the interrogators, preferably a direct transcript. Also the exact disposition made of this case, daily bulletins of progress on the alien hunt . . . yes, much.'

'My lord, I haven't the authority to—'

Brannoch gave him a name and address. 'Go to this fellow and explain the problem – at once. He'll tell you whom to get in touch with at the field and how to apply the right pressures.'

'My lord' – T'u Hayem wrung his hands – 'I thought perhaps, my lord . . . you know m-my wife—'

'I'll pay you the flat rate for this stuff, applied against your debts,' said Brannoch. 'If it turns out to be of some value, I'll consider a bonus. You may go.'

Silently, t'u Hayem bowed and backed out.

Brannoch sat motionless for a while after he was gone, and then ran through the series of stat-pictures. Good clear ones, page after page of writing in a language that was very strange to him. *Have to get this translated*, he thought, and the file cabinet in his brain gave the name of a scholar who would do it and keep a closed mouth.

He lounged a bit longer, then rose and went to the north wall of the room. It showed a moving stereo-pattern, very conventional; but behind it was a tank of hydrogen, methane, and ammonia at a thousand atmospheres pressure and minus one hundred degrees temperature, and there was visual and aural apparatus.

'Hello, you Thrymkas,' he said genially. 'Were you watching?'

'I was,' said the mechanical voice. Whether it was Thrymka-1, -2, -3, or -4 which spoke, Brannoch didn't know, nor did it matter. 'We are all in linkage now.'

'What do you think?'

'Apparently this alien has telekinetic powers,' said the monsters unemotionally. 'We assume these to be simply over electronic flows, because it is noted that everything he controlled or disabled involved electronic tubes. Only a small amount of telekinetic energy would be needed to direct the currents in vacuum as he wished and thus to take over the whole device.

'With high probability, this means that he is telepathic to some degree: sensitive to electrical and other neural pulses and capable of inducing such currents in the nervous systems of others. However, he could hardly have read the minds of his guards. Thus his action was probably just to remain free until he could evaluate his situation; but what he will then do is unpredictable until more is known of his psychology.'

'Yeah. That's what I thought, too,' said Brannoch. 'How about the ship – any ideas?'

'Verification must await translation of those documents, but it seems probable that the ship is not from some lost colony but from Earth herself – the remote past. In the course of wanderings, it chanced on the planet of this alien and took him along. The distance of said planet depends on the age of the ship, but since that seems to date from about five thousand years ago, the planet cannot be more than twenty-five hundred light-years removed.'

'Far enough,' said Brannoch. 'The known universe only reaches a couple of hundred.'

He took a turn about the room, hands clasped behind his back. 'I doubt that the humans matter,' he said, 'Especially if they really did come from Earth; then they're only of historical interest. But this alien, now – that electron-control effect is a new phenomenon. Just imagine what a weapon!' His eyes blazed. 'Put the enemy guns out of action, even turn them on their owners – disable the Technon itself— Father!'

'The same thought has doubtless occurred to the Solar authorities,' said the Thrymans.

'Uh-huh. Which is why they're pressing the hunt so hard.

If they don't catch him, these human friends of his may know how to do it. Even if they do make the capture, he's still likely to be influenced by his crewmates. Which makes the fellow of more importance than I'd realized—' Brannoch prowled the floor, turning the fact over in his mind.

All at once, he felt very alone. He had his aides here, his bodyguard, his agents, his spy ring, but they were few among the hostile billions of Sol. It would take almost four and a half years to get a message home . . . as long for the fleet to come here—

Sharp within him rose the image of his home. The steep, windy mountains of Thor, whistling stormy skies, heath and forest and broad fair plains, gray seas rolling under the tidal drag of three moons, the dear hard pull of the planet's mass; the hall of his ancestors, stone and timber rearing heavily to smoky rafters and ancient battle flags, his horses and hounds and the long halloo of hunting; the proud quarrelsome nobles, the solid, slow-spoken yeomen; great hush of winter snowfall and the first green flames of spring – the love and longing for his planet was an ache within his breast.

But he was a ruler, and the road of kings is hard. Also, and here he grinned, it would be fun to sack Earth, come the day.

His mission had suddenly narrowed. He had to get this alien for Centauri, so the scientists back home could study the power and duplicate it in a military unit. Failing that, he had to prevent Sol from doing the same – by killing the creature if necessary. He dismissed the idea of joining the chase with his own agents: too much of a giveaway, too small a chance of success. No, it would be better to work through those human prisoners.

But what hold could he get on men whose world was five thousand years in its grave?

Returning to the scanner, he went back through its spool. Some of the frames showed pictures and other objects which must be of a personal nature. There was one photograph of a woman which was quite excellent.

An idea occurred to him. He walked back onto the balcony, picked up his wineglass, and toasted the morning with a small laugh. Yes, it was a fine day.

CHAPTER THREE

LANGLEY sat up with a gasp and looked around him. He was alone.

For a moment, then, he sat very still, allowing memory and thought to enter him in a trickle. The whole pattern was too shatteringly big to be grasped at once.

Earth, altered almost beyond recognition: no more polar caps, the seas encroaching miles on every shore, unknown cities, unknown language, unknown men – there was only one answer, but he thrust it from him in a near panic.

There had been the landing, Saris Hronna's stunningly swift escape (why?), and then he and his companions had been separated. There were men in blue who spoke to him in a room full of enigmatic machines that whirred and clicked and blinked. One of those had been switched on and darkness had followed. Beyond that, there was only a dreamlike confusion of half-recalled voices. And now he was awake again, and naked, and alone.

Slowly, he looked at the cell. It was small, bare save for the couch and washstand which seemed to grow out of the green-tinted, soft and rubbery floor. There was a little ventilator grille in the wall, but no door that he could see.

He felt himself shaking, and fought for control. He wanted to weep, but there was a dry hollowness in him.

Peggy, he thought. *They could at least have left me your picture. It's all I'll ever have, now.*

A crack appeared in the farther wall, dilated until it was a doorway, and three men stepped through. The jerk which brought Langley erect told him how strained his nerves were.

He crouched back, trying to grasp the details of appearance on these strangers. It was hard, somehow. They were of another civilization, clothes and bodies and the very expressions were something new, a total gestalt was lacking for him.

Two of them were giants, nearly seven feet tall, their muscled bodies clad in a tight-fitting black uniform, their heads shaven. It took a little while to realize that the wide brown faces were identical. Twins?

The third was a little below average height, lithe and graceful. He wore a white tunic, deep-blue cloak, soft buskins on his feet, and little else; but the insigne on his breast, a sunburst with an eye, was the same as that of the two huge men behind him. He shared their smooth tawny skin, high cheekbones, faintly slanted eyes; but straight black hair was sleeked over the round head, and the face was handsome – broad low forehead, brilliant dark eyes, snub nose, strong chin, a wide full mouth, overall a nervous mobility.

All three bore holstered sidearms.

Langley had a sense of helplessness and degradation in standing nude before them. He tried for a poker face and an easy stance, but doubted that it was coming off. There was a thick lump as of unshed tears in his throat.

The leader inclined his head slightly. 'Captain Edward Langley,' he said, pronouncing it with a heavy accent. His voice was low, resonant, a superbly controlled instrument.

'Yes.'

'I take it that means *sya*.' The stranger was speaking the foreign tongue, and Langley understood it as if it had been his own. It was a clipped, rather high-pitched language, inflectional but with a simple and logical grammar. Among so much else, Langley felt only a vague surprise at his own knowledge, a certain relief at not having to study. 'Permit me to introduce myself. I am Minister Chanthavar Tang vo Lurin, chief field operative of the Solar militechnic intelligence corps and, I hope, your friend.'

Langley's brain felt thick, but he tried to analyze what had been said, calling on his new linguistic training. There were three forms of address, toward superiors, inferiors, and equals; Chanthavar was using the last, a courteous noncommittal gesture. His family name would be 'vo Lurin,' the prefix a sign of aristocratic birth as *von* and *de* had once been in Langley's world; however, only the lower ranks of the nobility were addressed by their surnames, the upper crust went by the given ones like ancient kings.

'Thank you, sir,' he answered stiffly.

'You must pardon such impoliteness as we may have shown you,' said Chanthavar with an oddly winning smile. 'Your comrades are safe, and you will soon rejoin them. However, as a spaceman you realize that we could not take chances with a complete stranger.'

He gestured to one of the guards, who laid a suit of clothes on the couch: similar to Chanthavar's, though lacking the military symbol and the jeweled star which he bore. 'If you will put these on, captain, it is the standard dress of the freeborn, and I'm afraid you'd feel too conspicuous in your own.'

Langley obeyed. The material was soft and comfortable. Chanthavar showed him how to close the fastenings, which seemed to be a kind of modified zipper. Then he sat down companionably on the bed, waving Langley to join him. The guards remained rigid by the door.

'Do you know what has happened to you?' he asked.

'I . . . think so,' said Langley dully.

'I'm sorry to tell you this.' Chanthavar's voice was gentle. 'Your log has been translated, so I know you didn't realize how the superdrive actually operates. Curious that you shouldn't, if you could build one.'

'There was an adequate theory,' said Langley. 'According to it, the ship warped through hyperspace.'

'There's no such animal. (Chanthavar's expression was literally: "That engine is drained.") Your theory was wrong, as must have been discovered very soon. Actually, a ship is projected as a wave pattern, re-forming at the point of destination; it's a matter of setting up harmonics in the electronic wave trains such that they reconstitute the original relationship at another point of space-time. Or so the specialists tell me, I don't pretend to understand the mathematics. Anyhow, there's no time of passage for those aboard, but according to an external observer, the trip is still made only at the speed of light. No better system has ever been found, and I doubt that it ever will. The nearest star, Alpha Centauri, is still nearly four and a half years away.'

'We'd have known that,' said Langley bitterly, 'except for the trouble with the space positioning. Because of that, it took us so long to find our test rockets that we had no way of observing that a finite time of passage had gone by. On my own voyage, the time lag was lost in the uncertainty of exact stellar positions. No wonder we had such trouble approaching Earth as we come home – it was moving in its own orbit, so was the sun, and we didn't know that— Home!' he exploded, with a stinging in his eyes. 'We crossed a total of some five thousand light-years. So it must be that many years later we came back.'

Chanthavar nodded.

'I don't suppose—' Langley had little hope, but: 'I don't suppose you have a way to send us back – into the past?'

'I'm sorry, no,' said Chanthavar. 'Time travel isn't even a theoretical possibility. We've done things which I believe were unknown in your time: gravity control, genetic engineering, making Mars and Venus and the Jovian moons habitable, oh, a great deal no doubt; but that is one art nobody will ever master.'

You can't go home again.

Langley asked wearily: 'What's happened in all that time?'

Chanthavar shrugged. 'The usual. Overpopulation, vanishing natural resources, war, famine, pestilence, depopulation, collapse, and then the resumption of the cycle. I don't think you'll find people very different today.'

'Couldn't you have taught me—?'

'Like the language? Not very well. That was a routine hypnotic process, quite automatic and not involving the higher centers of the brain. You were interrogated in that state too, but as for your more complex learning, it's best done gradually.'

There was a deadness in Langley, a stricken indifference, and he twisted away from it by trying to focus his mind on detail. Anything, just so it was impersonal enough. 'What kind of world is it now? And what can I do in it?'

Chanthavar leaned forward, elbows on knees, cocking a sidewise eye at the other. Langley forced himself to pay attention. 'Let's see. Interstellar emigration began about your time – not too extensive at first, because of the limitations of the superdrive and the relative scarcity of habitable planets. During later periods of trouble, there were successive waves of such outward movement, but most of these were malcontents and refugees who went far from Sol lest they be found later, and have been lost track of. We presume there are many of these lost colonies, scattered throughout the galaxy, and that some of them must have evolved into very different civilizations; but the universe we actually know something about and have even an indirect contact with, only reaches a couple of hundred light-years. Who would have any reason to explore farther?

'The ... let's see, I think it was the twenty-eighth world war which reduced the Solar System almost to barbarism and wiped out the colonies on the nearest stars. Reconstruction took a long time, but about two thousand years ago the Solar System was unified under the Technate, and this has endured so far. Colonization was resumed, with the idea of keeping the colonists fairly close to home and thus under control, while the emigration would be a safety valve for getting rid of those who didn't adjust well to the new arrangements.

'Of course, it didn't work. Distances are still too great; different environments inevitably produce different civilizations, other ways of living and thinking. About a thousand years ago, the colonies broke loose, and after a war we had to recognize their independence. There are about a dozen such states now with which we have fairly close contact – the League of Alpha Centauri is much the most powerful of them.

'If you want to know more about outer-space conditions, you can talk to a member of the Commercial Society. At present, though, I wouldn't bother, not till you're better up on modern Earth.'

'Yes, how about that?' said Langley. 'What is this Technate system, anyway?'

'The Technon is merely a giant sociomathematical computer which is fed all available data continuously, by all agencies, and makes basic policy decisions in view of them. A machine is less fallible, less selfish, less bribeable, than a man.' Chanthavar grinned. 'Also, it saves men the trouble of thinking for themselves.'

'I get the impression of an aristocracy—'

'Oh, well, if you want to call it that, somebody has to take responsibility for executing the Technon's policies and making the small daily decisions. The class of Ministers exists for that purpose. Under them are the Commoners. It's hereditary, but not so rigid that occasional recruits from the Commons don't get elevated to the Ministry.'

'Where I come from,' said Langley slowly, 'we'd learned better than to leave leadership to chance – and heredity is mighty chancy.'

'Not enough to matter nowadays. I told you we had genetic engineering.' Chanthavar laid a hand on his, squeezing slightly: it was not a feminine gesture, Langley realized, only a custom different from his. 'Look here, captain, I don't give a damn what you say, but some people get rather stuffy about it. Just a hint.'

'What can we . . . my friends and I . . . do?' Langley felt a dim annoyance at the strain in his voice.

'Your status is a bit unusual, isn't it? I'm appointing myself your patron, and you'll have a sort of quasi-Ministerial rank with funds of your own for the time being. Not charity, by the way; the Technate does have a special cash-box for unforeseen details, and you are hereby classified as an unforeseen detail. Eventually we'll work out something, but don't worry about getting sent to the commons. If nothing else, your knowledge of the past is going to make you the pet of the historians for the rest of your lives.'

Langley nodded. It didn't seem to matter much, one way or another. Peggy was dead.

Peggy was dead. For five thousand years she had been dust, darkness in her eyes and mold in her mouth, for five thousand years she had not been so much as a memory. He had held back the realization, desperately focusing himself on the unimportant details of survival, but it was entering him now like a knife.

He would never see her again.

And the child was dust, and his friends were dust, and his nation was dust; a world of living and laughter, proud buildings, song and tears and dreams, had sunk to a few ashen pages in some forgotten archive. And this was how it felt to be a ghost.

He bowed his head and wanted to weep, but there were eyes on him.

'It's no fun,' said Chanthavar sympathetically. After a moment: 'Take my advice and concentrate on immediate things for a while. That ought to help.'

'Yes,' said Langley, not looking at him.

'You'll strike roots here, too.'

'I wonder.'

'Well, you're better off if you don't, anyway.' An odd, bitter note there. 'Enjoy yourself. I'll show you some interesting dives.'

Langley stared at the floor.

'There's one thing you can help me with right now,' said Chanthavar. 'It's the reason I came here to see you, instead of having you sent to my office. More privacy.'

Langley touched his lips, remembering how Peggy's had brushed them and then clung to them, fifty centuries ago.

'It's about that alien you had along – Saris Hronna, was that the name you recorded for him?'

'More or less. What about him?'

'He escaped, you know. We haven't found him yet. Is he dangerous?'

'I don't think so, unless he gets too annoyed. His people do have a keen hunting instinct, but they're peaceable otherwise, treated us with great friendliness. Saris came along to see Earth, and as a kind of ambassador. I think he only broke away till he could get some idea of the situation. He must have dreaded the possibility of being caged.'

'He can control electronic and magnetronic currents. You know that?'

'Of course. It surprised us, too, at first. His race isn't telepathic in the usual sense, but they're sensitive to neural currents – especially emotions – and can project the same. I ... I really don't know whether he can read a human mind or not.'

T—B

'We have to find him,' said Chanthavar. 'Have you any idea where he might go, what he might do?'

'I'd ... have to think about it. But I'm sure he isn't dangerous.' Langley wondered, inside himself. He knew so little about the Holatan mind. It wasn't human. How would Saris Hronna react when he learned?

'You note their planet as being some thousand light-years from Sol. It's unknown to us, of course. We don't intend this being any harm, but we have to locate him.'

Langley glanced up. Under the mobile, smiling mask of his face, Chanthavar seemed almost feverish. There was a hunter's gleam in his eyes. 'What's the hurry?' asked the spaceman.

'Several things. Chiefly, the possibility that he may carry some germ to which man has no immunity. We've had plagues like that before.'

'We were on Holat a couple of months. I've never been healthier in my life.'

'Nevertheless, it has to be checked. Furthermore, how's he going to live except by robbery? Can't have that, either. Haven't you *any* idea where he might have gone?'

Langley shook his head. 'I'll think hard about it,' he said cautiously. 'Maybe I'll figure out an answer, but I can't promise anything.'

'Well,' said Chanthavar wryly, 'that'll have to do for now. Come on, let's get some dinner.'

He rose, Langley followed him out, and the two guards fell into step behind. The spaceman paid little attention to the halls and the anti-gravity rise-shafts along which he went. He was wrapped in his own desolation.

O my darling, I never came back. You waited, and you grew old, and you died, and I never came back to you. I ... I'm sorry, dearest of all, I'm sorry. Forgive me, O dust.

And down underneath, sharp and cold, a thought of wariness and suspicion: Chanthavar seemed pleasant enough. But he was top brass. Why should he take personal charge of the hunt for Saris? His reasons were thin – somewhere the real one lay hidden.

And what should I do about it?

CHAPTER FOUR

THERE was a party in the home of Minister Yulien, high commissioner of metallurgics; the cream of Solar and foreign society would be there, and Chanthavar brought the *Explorer* crew along.

Langley accompanied the agent down tall, columned passages where the air glowed with a soft light and murals traced shifting patterns on the gleaming walls. Behind him sat half a dozen bodyguards, identical giants. Chanthavar had explained that they were his personal slaves and the result of chromosome duplication in an exogenesis tank. There was something not quite human about them.

The spaceman was getting over his feeling of awkwardness, though he still couldn't imagine that he looked like much with hairy skinny legs sticking out from under his tunic. He, Blaustein, and Matsumoto had hardly been out of their palace suite in the day since they were released. They had sat around, saying little, now and then cursing in a whisper full of pain; it was still too new, too devastatingly sudden. They accepted Chanthavar's invitation without great interest. What business did three ghosts have at a party?

The suite was luxurious enough, furniture that molded itself to your contours and came when you called, a box which washed and brushed and massaged you and finished up by blowing scent on your scrubbed hide, softness and warmth and pastel color everywhere you looked. Langley remembered checked oilcloth on a kitchen table, a can of beer in front of him and the Wyoming night outside and Peggy sitting near.

'Chanthavar,' he asked suddenly, 'do you still have horses?' There was a word for it in this Earthspeak they had taught him, so maybe—

'Why . . . I don't know.' The agent looked a bit surprised. 'Never saw one that I remember, outside of historicals. I believe they have some on . . . yes, on Thor for amusement, if not on Earth. Lord Brannoch has often bored his guests by talking about horses and dogs.'

Langley sighed.

'If there aren't any in the Solar System, you could have one synthesized,' suggested Chanthavar. 'They can make pretty good animals to order. Care to hunt a dragon some day?'

'Never mind,' said Langley.

'There'll be a lot of important people here tonight,' said Chanthavar. 'If you can entertain one of them enough, your fortune's made. Stay away from Lady Halin; her husband's jealous and you'd end up as a mind-blanked slave unless I wanted to make an issue of it. You needn't act too impressed by what you see . . . a lot of the younger intellectuals, especially, make rather a game of deriding modern society, and would be happy to have you bear them out. But avoid saying anything which could be construed as dangerous. Otherwise, just go ahead and have a good time.'

They were not walking: they sat on comfortable benches and let the moving floor carry them. Once they went up a gravity shaft, it was a rather eerie experience to ride on nothing. At the end of the trip, which Langley estimated as three miles, they came to a gateway flanked by artificial waterfalls, and got up and went in past armed guards in gilt livery.

The first impression Langley got was of sheer enormousness. The room must be half a mile in diameter, and it was a swirling blaze of flashing color, some thousands of guests perhaps. It seemed roofless, open to a soft night sky full of stars and the moon, but he decided there was an invisible dome on it. Under its dizzy height, the city was a lovely, glowing spectacle.

There was perfume in the air, just a hint of sweetness, and music came from some hidden source. Langley tried to listen, but there were too many voices. Nor did the music make sense, the very scale was different. He murmured *sotto voce* to Blaustein: 'Always did think there wasn't much written after Beethoven, and seems like I was right into the indefinite future, world without end.'

'Amen,' said the physicist. His thin, long-nosed face was bleak.

Chanthavar was introducing them to their host, who was unbelievably fat and purple but not without a certain strength in the small black eyes. Langley recalled the proper formulas by which a client of one Minister addressed and genuflected to another.

'Man from past, eh?' Yulien cleared his throat. 'Int'restin'. Most int'restin'. Have to have long talk with you sometime. Hrumph! How d'y' like it here?'

'It is most impressive, my lord,' said Matsumoto, poker-faced.

'Hm-m-m. Ha. Yes. Progress. Change.'

'The more things change, my lord,' ventured Langley, 'the more they remain the same.'

'Hmph. Haw! Yes.' Yulien turned to greet someone else.

'Well put, fellow. Well put indeed.' There was a laugh in the voice. Langley bowed to a thin young man with mottled cheeks. 'Here, have a drink.' A table went by, and he lifted two crystal goblets off it and handed one over. 'I've been wanting to meet you, ever since the word got around. I'm at the university here, doing an historical study. The common element in all the thinkers who've tried to correlate the arts with the general state of society.'

Chanthavar raised one eyebrow. His own severely simple dress was conspicuous against the jewels and embroideries which flickered around him. 'And have you reached any conclusions, my friend?' he asked.

'Certainly, sir. I've found twenty-seven books which agree that the virile, unconscious stage of culture produces the corresponding type of art, simple and powerful. Over-ornamentation, such as ours, reflects a decadent state where mind has overcome the world-soul.'

'Ah, so. Have you ever seen the work done in the early stages of settlement on Thor, when they were fighting nature and each other all the time and known as the roughest two-fisted tribe in the universe? The basic pattern is the most intricate looping of vines you ever saw. On the other hand, in the last days of the Martian hegemony they went in for a boxlike simplicity. Have you read Sardu's commentaries? Shimarrin's? Or the nine spools of the *Tthnic Study*?'

'Well . . . well, sir, I've got them on my list, but even with the robots to help there's so much to read and—'

Chanthavar, obviously enjoying himself, went on to cite contrary and mutually contradictory examples from the past three thousand years of history. Langley took the chance to fade out of the picture.

A rather good-looking woman with somewhat protuberant eyes grasped his arm and told him how *exciting* it was to *see* a man from the *past* and she was *sure* it had been such an *interesting* epoch back when they were so *virile*. Langley felt relieved when a sharp-faced oldster called her to him and she left in a pout. Clearly, women had a subservient position in the Technate, though Chanthavar had mentioned something about occasional great female leaders.

He slouched moodily toward a buffet, where he helped

himself to some very tasty dishes and more wine. How long would the farce go on, anyway? He'd rather have been off somewhere by himself.

It was summer outside. Always summer on Earth now, the planet had entered an interglacial period with the help of man, more carbon dioxide in the air. With Peggy, this could have been a high and proud adventure; but Peggy was dead and forgotten. He wanted to go outside and walk on the earth to which she had returned, long and long ago.

A flabby person who had had a bit too much to drink threw an arm around his neck and bade him welcome and started asking him about the bedroom techniques of his period. It would have been a considerable relief to— Langley unclenched his fists.

'Want some girls? Min'ster Yulien most hospitable, come right this way, have li'l fun 'fore the Centaurians blow us all to dust.'

'That's right,' jeered a younger man. 'That's why we're going to have the hide beaten off us. People like you. Could they fight in your time, Captain Langley?'

'Tolerable well, when we had to,' said the American.

'That's what I thought. Survivor types. You conquered the stars because you weren't afraid to kick the next man. We are. We've gotten soft, here in the Solar System. Haven't fought a major war in a thousand years, and now that one's shaping up we don't know how.'

'Are you in the army?' asked Langley.

'I?' The young fellow looked surprised. 'The Solar military forces are slaves. Bred and trained for the job, publicly owned. The higher officers are Ministers, but—'

'Well, would you advocate drafting your own class into service?'

'Wouldn't do any good. They aren't fit. Not in a class with the slave specialists. The Centaurians, though, they call up their free-born, and they *like* fighting. If we could learn that too—'

'Son,' asked Langley recklessly, 'have you ever seen men with their heads blown open, guts coming out, ribs sticking through the skin? Ever faced a man who intended to kill you?'

'No . . . no, of course not. But—'

Langley shrugged. He'd met this type before, back home. He mumbled an excuse and got away. Blaustein joined him, and they fell into English. 'Where's Bob?' asked Langley.

Blaustein gave a crooked grin.

'Last I saw, he was heading off-stage with one of the female entertainers. Nice-looking little piece, too. Maybe he's got the right idea.'

'For him,' said Langley.

'I can't. Not now, anyway.' Blaustein looked sick. 'You know, I thought maybe, even if everything we knew is gone, the human race would finally have learned some sense. I was a pacifist, you know – intellectual pacifist, simply because I could see what a bloody, brainless farce it was, how nobody gained anything except a few smart boys—' Blaustein was a little drunk, too. 'And the solution is so easy! It stares you right in the face. A universal government with teeth. That's all. No more war. No more men getting shot and resources plundered and little children burned alive. I thought maybe in five thousand years even this dim-witted race of ours would get that lesson hammered home. Remember, they've never had a war at all on Holat. Are we that much stupider?'

'I should think an interstellar war would be kind of hard to fight,' said Langley. 'Years of travel just to get there.'

'Uh-huh. Also, little economic incentive. If a planet can be colonized at all, it's going to be self-sufficient. Those two reasons are why there hasn't been a real war for a thousand years, since the colonies broke loose.'

Blaustein leaned closer, weaving a trifle on his feet. 'But there's one shaping up now. We may very well see it. Rich mineral resources on the planets of Sirius, and the government there weak, and Sol and Centauri strong. Both of them want those planets. Neither can let the other have them, it'd be too advantageous. I was just talking to an officer, who put it in very nearly those words, besides adding something about the Centaurians being filthy barbarians.'

'So I'd still like to know how you fight across four-plus light-years,' said Langley.

'You send a king-size fleet, complete with freighters full of supplies. You meet the enemy fleet and whip it in space. Then you bombard the enemy planets from the sky. Did you know they can disintegrate any kind of matter completely now? Nine times ten to the twentieth ergs per gram. And there are things like synthetic virus and radioactive dust. You smash civilization on those planets, land, and do what you please. Simple. The only thing to be sure of is that the enemy fleet doesn't beat you, because then your own home is lying wide open. Sol and Centauri have been intriguing, sparring, for decades now. As soon as one of them gets a clear advantage – wham! Fireworks.' Blaustein gulped his wine and reached for more.

'Of course,' he said owlishly, 'there's always the chance that even if you beat the enemy, enough of his ships will escape to go to your home system and knock out the planetary defenses and bombard. Then you have two systems gone back to the caves. But when has that prospect ever stopped a politician? Or psychotechnical administrator, as I believe they call 'em now. Lemme alone. I want to get blotto.'

Chanthavar found Langley a few minutes later and took him by the arm. 'Come,' he said. 'His Fidelity, the chief of the Technon Servants, wants to meet you. His Fidelity is a very important man . . . Excellent Sulon, may I present Captain Edward Langley?'

He was a tall and thin old man in a plain blue robe and cowl. His lined face was intelligent, but there was something humorless and fanatical about his mouth. 'This is interesting,' he said harshly. 'I understand that you wandered far in space, captain.'

'Yes, my lord.'

'Your documents have already been presented to the Technon. Every scrap of information, however seemingly remote, is valuable: for only through sure knowledge of all the facts can the machine make sound decisions. You would be surprised how many agents there are whose only job is the constant gathering of data. The state thanks you for your service.'

'It is nothing, my lord,' said Langley with due deference.

'It may be much,' said the priest. 'The Technon is the foundation of Solar civilization; without it, we are lost. Its very location is unknown to all save the highest ranks of my order, its servants. For this we are born and raised, for this we renounce all family ties and worldly pleasures. We are so conditioned that if an attempt is made to get our secrets from us, and there is no obvious escape, we die – automatically. I tell you this to give you some idea of what the Technon means.'

Langley couldn't think of any response. Sulon was proof that Sol hadn't lost all vitality, but there was an inhumanness over him.

'I am told that an extraterrestrial being of unknown race was with your crew, and has escaped,' went on the old man. 'I must take a very grave view of this. He is a completely unpredictable factor – your own journal gives little information.'

'I'm sure he's harmless, my lord,' said Langley.

'That remains to be seen. The Technon itself orders that he be found or destroyed immediately. Have you, as an acquaintance of his, any idea of how to go about this?'

There it was again. Langley felt cold. The problem of Saris Hronna had all the VIPs – the VGDIPs – scared sweatless; and a frightened man can be a vicious creature.

'Standard search patterns haven't worked,' said Chant-havar. 'I'll tell you this much, though it's secret: he killed three of my men and got away in their flier. Where has he gone?'

'I'll . . . have to think,' stammered Langley. 'This is most unfortunate, my lord. Believe me, I'll give it all my atten-tion, but – you can lead a horse to water, but you can't make him drink.'

Chanthavar smiled; the cliché, dead and now resurrected, amused him, and Langley thought what a reputation he could get for himself by merely cribbing from Shaw, Wilde, Leacock— Sulon said stiffly: 'This horse had better drink, sir, and soon,' and dismissed them with a nod. Chanthavar saw an acquaintance and plunged into a hot argument on the proper way to mix some kind of drink called a re-cycler.

Langley was pulled away by a plump, hairy hand. It be-longed to a large pot-bellied man in foreign-looking dress: gray robe and slippers, loops of diamond and rubies. The head was massive, with an elephantine nose, disorderly flame-red hair and the first beard Langley had seen in this age, surprisingly keen light eyes. The rather high voice was accented, an intonation not of Earth: 'Greeting, sir. I have been most anxious to meet you. Goltam Valti is the name.'

'Your servant, my lord,' said Langley.

'No, no. I've no title. Poor old greasy lickspittle Goltam Valti is not to the colors born. I'm of the Commercial Society, and we don't have nobles. Can't afford 'em. Hard enough to make an honest living these days, with buyers and sellers alike grudging you enough profit to eat on, and one's dear old homestead generations away. Well, about a decade in my case, I'm from Ammon in the Tau Ceti system orig-inally. A sweet planet, that, with golden beer and a lovely girl to serve it to you, ah, yes!'

Langley felt a stirring of interest. He'd heard something about the Society, but not enough. Valti led him to a divan and they sat down and whistled at a passing table for refreshments.

'I'm chief factor at Sol,' continued Valti. 'You must come see our building sometime. Souvenirs of a hundred planets there, I'm sure it'll interest you. But five thousand years' worth of wandering, that is too much even for a trader. You must have seen a great deal, captain, a great deal. Ah, were I young again—'

Langley threw subtlety aside and asked a few straightforward questions. Getting information out of Valti took patience, you had to listen to a paragraph of self-pity to get a sentence worth hearing, but something emerged. The Society had existed for a thousand years or more, recruited from all planets, even non-human races: it carried on most of the interstellar trade there was, goods which were often from worlds unknown to this little section of the galaxy. Luxuries chiefly, exotic things, but there were also important industrial materials involved, an item which was growing as the civilized planets used up their own resources. For Society personnel, the great spaceships were home, men and women and children living their lives on them. They had their own laws, customs, language, they owed allegiance to no one else. 'A civilization in its own right, Captain Langley, a horizontal civilization cutting across the proudly vertical ones rooted on the planets, and in its poor way outliving them all.'

'Haven't you a capital – a government—'

'Details, my friend, details we can discuss later. Do come see me, I am a lonely old man. Perhaps I can offer you some small entertainment. Did you by any chance stop in the Tau Ceti system? No? That's a shame, it would have interested you, the double ring system of Osiris and the natives of Horus and the beautiful, beautiful valleys of Ammon, yes, yes.' The names originally given to the planets had changed, also within the Solar System, but not so much that Langley could not recognize what mythical figures the discoverers had had in mind. Valti went on to reminisce about worlds he had seen in the lost lamented days of his youth, and Langley found it an enjoyable conversation.

'Ho, there!'

Valti jumped up and bowed wheezily. 'My lord! You honor me beyond my worth. It has been overly long since I saw you.'

'All of two weeks,' grinned the blond giant in the screaming crimson jacket and blue trousers. He had a wine goblet in one brawny hand, the other held the ankles of a tiny, exquisite dancing girl who perched on his shoulder and squealed with laughter. 'And then you diddled me out of a thousand solars, you and your loaded dice.'

'Most excellent lord, fortune must now and then smile even on my ugly face; the probability-distribution curve demands it.' Valti made washing motions with his hands. 'Perhaps my lord would care for revenge some evening next week?'

'Could be. Whoops!' The giant slid the girl to earth and dismissed her with a playful thwack. 'Run along, Thura, Kolin, whatever your name is. I'll see you later.' His eyes were very bright and blue on Langley. 'Is this the dawn man I've been hearing about?'

'Yes – my lord, may I present Captain Edward Langley? Lord Brannoch dhu Crombar, the Centaurian ambassador.'

So this was one of the hated and feared men from Thor. He and Valti were the first recognizably Caucasoid types the American had seen in this age: presumably their ancestors had left Earth before the races had melted into an almost uniform stock here, and possibly environmental factors had had something to do with fixing their distinctive features.

Brannoch grinned jovially, sat down, and told an uproariously improper story. Langley countered with the tale of the cowboy who got three wishes, and Brannoch's guffaw made glasses tremble.

'So you still used horses?' he asked afterward.

'Yes, my lord. I was raised in horse country – we used them in conjunction with trucks. I was ... going to raise them myself.'

Brannoch seemed to note the pain in the spaceman's voice, and with a surprising tact went on to describe his stable at home. 'I think you'd like Thor, captain,' he finished. 'We still have elbow room. How they can breathe with twenty billion hunks of fat meat in the Solar System, I'll never know. Why not come see us sometime?'

'I'd like to, my lord,' said Langley, and maybe he wasn't being entirely a liar.

Brannoch sprawled back, letting his interminable legs stretch across the polished floor. 'I've kicked around a bit, too,' he said. 'Had to get out of the system a while back, when my family got the short end of a feud. Spent a hundred years external time knocking around, till I got a chance to make a comeback. Planetography's a sort of hobby with me, which is the only reason I come to your parties, Valti, you kettle-bellied old fraud. Tell me, Captain, did you ever touch at Procyon?'

For half an hour the conversation spanned stars and planets. Something of the weight within Langley lifted. The vision of many-faced strangeness spinning through an endless outer dark was one to catch at his heart.

'By the way,' said Brannoch, 'I've been hearing some rumors about an alien you had along, who broke loose. What's the truth on that?'

'Ah, yes,' murmured Valti in his tangled beard. 'I, too, have been intrigued, yes, a most interesting sort he seems to be. Why should he take such a desperate action?'

Langley stiffened. What had Chanthavar said – wasn't the whole affair supposed to be confidential?

Brannoch would have his spies, of course; and seemingly Valti did, too. The American had a chilling sense of immense contending powers, a machine running wild and he caught in the whirling gears.

'I'd rather like to add him to the collection,' said Brannoch idly. 'That is, not to harm him, just to meet the creature. If he really is a true telepath, he's almost unique.'

'The Society would also have an interest in this matter,' said Valti diffidently. 'The planet may have something to trade worth even such a long trip.'

After a moment, he added dreamily: 'I think the payment for such information would be quite generous, captain. The Society has its little quirks, and the desire to meet a new race is one. Yes . . . there would be money in it.'

'Could be I'd venture a little fling myself,' said Brannoch. 'Couple million solars – and my protection. These are troubled times, captain. A powerful patron isn't to be sniffed at.'

'The Society,' remarked Valti, 'has extraterritorial rights. It can grant sanctuary, as well as removal from Earth, which is becoming an unsalubrious place. And, of course, monetary rewards – three million solars, as an investment in new knowledge?'

'This is hardly the place to talk business,' said Brannoch. 'But as I said, I think you might like Thor – or we could set you up anywhere else you chose. Three and a half million.'

Valti groaned. 'My lord, do you wish to impoverish me? I have a family to support.'

'Yeah. One on each planet,' chuckled Brannoch.

Langley sat very still. He thought he knew why they all wanted Saris Hronna – but what to do about it?

Chanthavar's short supple form emerged from the crowd. 'Oh, there you are,' he said. He bowed casually to Brannoch and Valti. 'Your servant, my lord and good sir.'

'Thanks, Channy,' said Brannoch. 'Sit down, why don't you?'

'No. Another person would like to meet the captain. Excuse us.'

When they were safely into the mob, Chanthavar drew Langley aside. 'Were those men after you to deliver this alien up to them?' he asked. There was something ugly on his face.

'Yes,' said Langley wearily.

'I thought so. The Solar government's riddled with their agents. Well, don't do it.'

A tired, harried anger bristled in Langley. 'Look here, son,' he said, straightening till Chanthavar's eyes were well below his, 'I don't see as how I owe any faction today anything. Why don't you quit treating me like a child?'

'I'm not going to hold you incommunicado, though I could,' said Chanthavar mildly. 'Isn't worth the trouble, because we'll probably have that beast before long. I'm just warning you, though, that if he should fall into any hands but mine, it'll go hard with you.'

'Why not lock me up and be done with it?'

'It wouldn't make you think, as I'll want you to think in case my own search fails. And it's too crude.' Chanthavar paused, then said with a curious intensity: 'Do you know why I play out this game of politics and war? Do you think maybe I want power for myself? That's for fools who want to command other fools. It's fun to play, though – life gets so thundering tedious otherwise. What else can I do that I haven't done a hundred times already? But it's fun to match wits with Brannoch and that slobbering red-beard. Win, lose, or draw, it's amusing; but I intend to win.'

'Ever thought of – compromising?'

'Don't let Brannoch bluff you. He's one of the coldest and cleverest brains in the galaxy. Fairly decent sort – I'll be sorry when I finally have to kill him – but— Never mind!' Chanthavar turned away. 'Come on, let's get down to the serious business of getting drunk.'

CHAPTER FIVE

THERE was darkness around Saris Hronna where he crouched, and a wet wind blowing off the canal with a thousand odors of strangeness. The night was full of fear.

He lay in the weeds and mud of the canal bank, flattening his belly to the earth, and listened for those who hunted him.

There was no moon yet, but the stars were high and clear, a distant pulsing glow on the world's edge told of a city, and for him there was enough gray light for vision. He looked down the straight line of the canal, the ordered rows of wind-rustling grain marching from horizon to horizon, the rounded bulk of somebody's darkened hut three miles off; his nostrils sucked in a cool dank air, green growth and the small warm scurry of wildlife; he heard the slow, light dragging of wind, the remote honking of a bird, the incredibly faint boom of some airship miles overhead; his nerves drank the eddies and pulses of other nerves, other beings – so had he lain in the darknesses of Holat, waiting for an animal he hunted to come by, and letting himself flow into the vast murmurous midnight. But this time he was the quarry, and he could not blend himself to the life of Earth. It was too alien: every smell, every vision, every trembling nerve-current of mouse or beetle, was saw-toothed with strangeness; the very wind blew with another voice.

Below his waiting and his fear, there was a gape of sorrow. Somehow he had gone through time as well as space, somehow the planet he knew and all his folk, mate and cubs and kindred, were a thousand years behind him. He was alone as none of his race had ever been alone. Alone and, lonely.

The philosophers of Holat had been suspicious of that human ship, he remembered bleakly. In their world-view, the universe and every object and process within it were logically, inevitably finite. Infinity was a concept which violated some instinct of rightness when taken from pure mathematics into the physical cosmos, and the idea of crossing light-years in no time at all had not made sense.

The blinding sunburst newness of it all had overwhelmed ancient thought. It had been too much of a revelation, those beings from the sky and their ship; it had been too much fun, working with them, learning, finding answers to problems which their un-Holatan minds could not readily see. Caution went by the board for a while.

And as a result, Saris Hronna had fled through a forest like something out of a dream, dodging, ducking, pursued by bolts of energy which sizzled lightning-fashion in his tracks, twisting and turning and hiding with every hunter's trick he knew, to save a life which was ashen in his mouth.

His dog-teeth flashed white as the lips drew back. There was something to live for, even now. Something to kill for.

If he could get back— It was a thought like one dim candle in a huge and storming night. Holat would not have changed much, even in two thousand years, not unless some human ship had blundered on her again. His folk were not static, there was progress all the time, but it was a growth like evolution, in harmony with the seasons and the fields and the great rhythm of time. He could find himself again.

But—

Something stirred in the sky. Saris Hronna flattened himself as if he would dig into the mud. His eyes narrowed to yellow slits as he focused his mind-senses, straining into heaven for a ghost.

Yes: currents, and not animal but the cold swirl of electrons in vacuum and gas, an undead pulsation which was like a nail scraped along his nerves. It was a small aircraft, he decided, circling in a slow path, reaching out with detectors. It was hunting him.

Maybe he should have submitted meekly. The *Explorer*

humans were decent, for Langley he had a growing affection. Maybe these far kin of his were reasonable too— No! There was too much at hazard. There was his whole race.

They did not have this star-spanning technology on Holat. There it was still tools of bone and flint, travel on foot or in a dugout with sails and oars, food from hunting and fishing and the enormous herds of meat animals half-domesticated by telethymic control. One Holatan on the ground could track down a dozen men and kill them in the green stillness of his forests; but one human spaceship could hang in the sky and lash the planet with death.

The aircraft up there was moving away. Saris Hronna snapped after breath, filling his lungs again.

What to do, where to go, how to escape?

His mind shrieked to be a cub again, small and furry, lying on skins in a cave or sod hut and crowding against the dim vast form of mother. He thought with a sob of the days rolling and tumbling in sunlight, the snug winter nights when they couched underground – singing, talking, joining themselves in the great warm oneness of emotional communion – the times his father had taken him out to learn hunting, even his own turns at herding which had so bored him then. The small, isolated family group was the heart of his society, without it he was lost – and his clan was long dead now.

The aircraft was coming back. Its track was a spiral. How many of them were there, over how many miles of Earth's night?

His mind quivered, less from fear than from hurt and loneliness. The life of Holat was grounded in order, ceremony, the grave courtesies between old and young, male and female, the calm pantheistic religion, the rites of the family at morning and evening: everything in its place, balance, harmony, sureness, always the knowing that life was one enormous unity. And he had been pitched into the foreign dark and was being hounded like a beast.

The fixed pattern of life had not been onerous, because its tensions were released: in the chase and in the libertine orgies of the fairs where families met to trade, discuss plans and policies, mate off the youths, drink and make merry. But here, tonight—

The thing above was coming lower. Saris' muscles grew rigid, and there was a blaze in his heart. Let it come within range, and he would seize control and smash it into the ground!

He was not wholly unfitted for this moment of murder. There was no domination within a Holatan family, no harsh father or jibing brother, they were all one; and a member who showed real talent was ungrudgingly supported by the others while he worked at his art, or his music, or his thinking. Saris had been that kind, as he emerged from cubhood. Later he had gone to one of the universities.

There he herded cattle, made tools, swept floors, as fitting return for the privilege of lying in the hut of some philosopher or artist or woodworker, arguing with him and learning from him. His particular flair had been for the physical sciences.

They had their learning on Holat, he thought defensively as the metal death dropped slowly toward him. The books were hand-copied on parchment, but there was sound knowledge in them. Astronomy, physics, and chemistry were elementary beside man's, though correct as far as they went. Biological technique, the breeding of animals, the understanding and use of ecology, were at least equal in the areas where no instrument but a simple lens and scalpel were needed – possibly superior. And the mathematicians of Holat had an innate ability which towered above that of any human.

Saris remembered Langley's astonishment at how fast English was learned, at seeing half-grown cubs studying non-Euclidean geometry and the theory of functions. The man had gotten some glimpse of the various schools of philosophy, the lively discussion that went on between them, and had rather ruefully admitted that their rigorous logic, their highly developed semantics, their mutual grounding in a hard empirical common sense, made them more valuable tools than anything of the sort his race had ever produced. It had been a philosopher, the same who first clarified the relationship between discontinuous functions and ethics, who had suggested the key improvement in the *Explorer's* circuits.

The craft was hovering, as if it were a bird of prey readying to swoop. Still out of control range – they must have detectors, perhaps of infrared, which made them suspect his presence. He dared not move.

The safest thing for them to do would be to drop a bomb. Langley had told him about bombs. And that would be the end – a flash and roar he could not feel, dissolution, darkness forever.

Well, he thought, feeling how the slow sad wind ruffled his whiskers, he had little to complain of. It had been a good life. He had been one of the wandering scholars who drifted around the world, always welcomed for the news he could bring, always seeing something fresh in the diversity of basically similar cultures which dotted his planet. His sort bound a planet together. Lately he had settled down, begun a family, taught at the University of Sundance-Through-Rain – but if it came to swift death in an unknown land, life had still been kind.

No, no! He brought his mind up sharply. He could not die, not yet. Not until he knew more, knew that Holat was safe from these pale hairless monsters or knew how to warn and defend her. His muscles bunched to break and run.

The airship descended with a swiftness that sucked a gasp from him. He reached out to grasp the swirling electric and magnetic streams with the force-fields of his brain – and withdrew, shuddering.

No. Wait. There might be a better way.

The craft landed in the fields, a good hundred yards off. Saris gathered his legs and arms under him. How many were there?

Three. Two of them were getting out, the third staying inside. He couldn't see through the tall stand of grain, but he could sense that one of the two carried some kind of instrument which was not a weapon – a detector, then. Blind in the dark, they could still track him.

But, of course, they weren't sure it was Saris. Their instrument could just as well be registering a stray animal, or a man. He could smell the sharp adrenalin stink of their fear.

In a gliding rush, Saris Hronna went up the bank and four-legged through the grain.

Someone yelled. A bolt of energy snapped at him, the vegetation flamed up where it struck and ozone scorched his nostrils. His mind could not take care of the weapons, it had already clamped down on the engine and communicator of the vessel.

He hardly felt the beam which sizzled along his ribs, leaving a welt of burned flesh. Leaping, he was on the nearest man. The figure went down, his hands tore out its throat, and he sprang aside as the other one fired.

Someone cried out, a thin panicky wail in the darkness. A gun which threw a hail of lead missiles chattered from the boat's nose. Saris jumped, landing on the roof. The man remaining outside was flashing a light, trying to catch him in its ray. Coldly, the Holatan estimated distances. Too far.

He yowled, sliding to earth again as he did. The flashlight and a blaster beam stabbed where he had been. Saris covered the ground between in three leaps. Rising, he cuffed hard, and felt neck bones snap under his palm.

Now – the boat! Saris snuffled at the door. It was locked

against him, and the lock was purely mechanical, not to be controlled by the small energy output of his brain. He could feel the terror of the man huddled inside.

Well— He picked up one of the dropped blasters. For a moment he considered it, using the general principle that function determines form. The hand went around this grip, one finger squeezed this lever, the fire spat from the other end – that adjustment on the nose must regulate the size of the beam. He experimented and was gratified at having his deductions check out. Returning to the boat, he melted away its door lock.

The man within was backed against the farther wall, a gun in his hand, waiting with a dry scream in his throat for the devil to break through. Saris pinpointed him telepathically – aft of the entrance – good! Opening the door a crack, just enough to admit his hand, he fired around the edge of it. The blaster was awkward in a grasp the size of his, but one bolt was enough.

The smell of burned meat was thick around him. Now he had to work fast; there must be other craft in the vicinity. Collecting all the weapons, he hunched himself over the pilot's chair – it was too small for him to sit in – and studied the control panel.

The principle used was unfamiliar, something beyond the science of Langley's time. Nor could he read the symbols on the controls. But by tracing the electric currents and gyro-magnetic fields with his mind, and applying logic, he got a notion of how to operate the thing.

It rose a little clumsily as he maneuvered the switches, but he got the hang of it fast. Soon he was high in the sky, speeding through a darkness that whistled around him. One screen held an illuminated map with a moving red point that must represent his own location. Helpful.

He couldn't stay in this machine long, it would be identified and shot down. He must use it to get supplies and then to find a hiding place before dawn, after which it must —

fly westward to crash in the ocean. He should be able to adjust the automatic pilot to do that.

Where to go? What to do?

He needed some place where he could lie concealed and think, whence he could go forth to spy, to which he could return and make a stand if luck went against him. He needed time in which to learn and decide.

These humans were a strange race. He didn't understand them. He had talked much with Langley, there was a comradeship between them, but there had been things half-seen in Langley, too, which had crawled on his nerves. That near-religious concept of exploring all space, simply for its own sake – that wasn't Holatan. Aside from its pursuit of pure, abstract knowledge, the Holatan mind was not idealistic, it found something vaguely obscene in the picture of utter dedication to an impersonal cause.

These new humans who now held Earth might make a cause out of conquering Holat. The distance was enormous, but you never knew.

It might be safest and wisest to destroy their whole civilization, send them back to the caves. That was an ambitious project, probably too much to attempt; but surely he could do something, if only by playing one faction off against another. He had a pretty good notion already of why they were so anxious to catch or kill him.

He would have to wait, and observe, and think, before deciding on a course of deeds. That required a place in which to lie hidden, and he thought he knew where to go. It was worth trying, at least. He studied the unrolling map, comparing it with those of Langley's he had seen and put into a well-trained eidetic memory, translating the symbolism by correspondence and estimating the effects of five thousand years' change. Then he turned the boat northeastward and crouched down to wait.

CHAPTER SIX

PROGRESS does get made: Langley's refresher cabinet removed all trace of hangover from him the next morning, and the service robot slid breakfast from a chute onto a table and removed it when he was through. But after that there was a day of nothing to do but sit around and brood. Trying to shake off his depression, Langley dialed for books – a slave superintendent had shown him how to operate the gadgets in the apartment. The machine clicked to itself, hunted through the city library microfiles under the topics selected, and made copy spools which the spacemen put into the scanners.

Blaustein tried to read a novel, then some poetry, then some straight articles, and gave it up; with his scant knowledge of their background, they were almost meaningless. He did report that all writing today seemed highly stylized, the intricate form, full of allusions to the classic literature of two millennia ago, more important than the rather trivial content. 'Pope and Dryden,' he muttered in disgust, 'but they at least had something to say. What are you finding out, Bob?'

Matsumoto, who was trying to orient himself in modern science and technology, shrugged. 'Nothing. It's all written for specialists, takes for granted that the reader's got a thorough background. I'd have to go to college all over again to follow it – what the blue hell is a Zagan matrix? No popularization at all; guess nobody but the specialists care what makes things tick. All I get is an impression that nothing really new has been found out for a couple of thousand years.'

'Petrified civilization,' said Langley. 'They've struck a balance, everybody in his place, everything running smooth enough – there's been nothing to kick them out of their rut. Maybe the Centaurians ought to take over, I dunno.'

He returned to his own spools, history, trying to catch up on all that had happened. It was surprisingly hard. Nearly everything he found was a scholarly monograph assuming an immense erudition in a narrow field. Nothing for the common man, if that much misunderstood animal still existed. And the closer he got to the present, the fewer references there were – understandable enough, especially in a civilization whose future seemed all to lie behind it.

The most important discovery since the superdrive was, he gathered, the paramathematical theory of man, both as individual and as society, which had made it possible to reorganize on a stable, predictable, logical basis. There had been no guesswork on the part of the Technate's founders: they didn't think that such and such arrangements for production and distribution would work, they *knew*. The science wasn't perfect, it couldn't be; such eventualities as the colonial revolts had arisen unforeseen; but the civilization was stable, with high negative feedback, it adjusted smoothly to new conditions.

Too smoothly. The means of sound social organization had not been used to liberate man, but to clamp the yoke more tightly – for a small cadre of scientists had necessarily laid out the plans and seen them through, and they or their descendants (with fine, humane rationalizations they may even have believed themselves) had simply stayed in power. It was, after all, logical that the strong and the intelligent should rule – the ordinary man was simply not capable of deciding issues in a day when whole planets could be wiped clean of life. It was also logical to organize the rules; selective breeding, controlled heredity, psychological training, could produce a slave class which was both efficient and contented, and that too was logical. The ordinary man had not objected to such arrangements, indeed he had accepted them eagerly, because the concentration and centralization

of authority which had by and large been increasing ever
since the Industrial Revolution had inculcated him with a
tradition of subservience. He wouldn't have known what to
do with liberty if you gave it to him.

Langley wondered with a certain glumness whether any
other outcome would have been possible in the long run.

Chanthavar called up to suggest a tour of the city, Lora,
next day. 'I know you've found it pretty dull so far,' he
apologized, 'but I have much to do right now. I'd enjoy
showing you around tomorrow, though, and answering any
questions you may have. That seems the best way for you to
get yourselves oriented.'

When he had hung up, Matsumoto said: 'He doesn't seem
a bad guy. But if the setup here's as aristocratic as I think,
why should he take so much trouble personally?'

'We're something new, and he's bored,' said Blaustein.
'Anything for a novelty.'

'Also,' murmured Langley, 'he needs us. I'm pretty sure
he can't get anything very coherent out of us under hypnosis
or whatever they use nowadays, or we'd've been in the cala-
boose long ago.'

'You mean the Saris affair?' Blaustein hesitated. 'Ed,
have you any notion where that overgrown otter is and what
he's up to?'

'Not . . . yet,' said Langley. They were speaking English, but
he was sure there must be a recording microphone somewhere
in the room, and translations could be made. 'It beats me.'

Inwardly, he wondered why he held back. He wasn't cut
out for this world of plotting and spying and swift deadly
action. He never had been; a spaceman was necessarily a
gentle, introverted sort, unable to cope with the backbitings
and intrigues of office politics. In his own time, he had
always been able to pull rank when something went wrong –
and afterward lie awake wondering whether his judgment
had been fair and what the men really thought of him. Now
he was nothing.

It would be so easy to give in, cooperate with Chanthavar, and glide with the current. How did he know it wouldn't be right? The Technate seemed to represent order, civilization, justice of sorts; he had no business setting himself up against twenty billion people and five thousand years of history. Had Peggy been along, he would have surrendered, her neck was not one to risk for a principle he wasn't even sure of.

But Peggy was dead, and he had little except principle to live for. It was no fun playing God, even on this petty scale, but he had come from a society which laid on each man the obligation to decide things for himself.

Chanthavar called the following afternoon, still yawning. 'What a time to get up!' he complained. 'Life isn't worth the effort before sundown. Well, shall we go?'

As he led them out, half a dozen of his guards closed in around the party. 'What're they for, anyhow?' asked Langley. 'Protection against the Commons?'

'I'd like to see a Commoner even think about making trouble,' said Chanthavar. 'If he can think, which I sometimes doubt. No, I need these fellows against my own rivals. Brannoch, for instance, would gladly knock me off just to get an incompetent successor. I've ferreted out a lot of his agents. And then I have my competitors within the Technate. Having discovered that bribery and cabals won't unseat me, they may very well try the less subtle but direct approach.'

'What would they stand to gain by . . . assassinating you?' inquired Blaustein.

'Power, position, maybe some of my estates. Or they may be out and out enemies: I had to kick in a lot of teeth on my own way up, there aren't many influential offices these days. My father was a very petty Minister on Venus, my mother a Commoner concubine. I only got rank by passing certain tests and . . . elbowing a couple of half brothers aside. Chanthavar grinned. 'Rather fun. And the competition does keep my class somewhat on its toes, which is why the Technon allows it.'

They emerged on a bridgeway and let its moving belt carry them along, dizzily high over the city. At this altitude, Langley could see that Lora was built as a single integrated unit: no building stood alone, they were all connected, and there was a solid roof underneath decking over the lower levels. Chanthavar pointed to the misty horizon, where a single great tower reared skeletal. 'Weather-control station,' he said. 'Most of what you see belongs to the city, Ministerial public park, but over that way is the boundary of an estate belonging to Tarahoë. He raises grain on it, being a back-to-nature crank.'

'Haven't you any small farms?' asked Langley.

'Space, no!' Chanthavar looked surprised. 'They do on the Centaurian planets, but I'd find it hard to imagine a more inefficient system. A lot of our food is synthesized, the rest is grown on Ministerial lands – in fact, the mines and factories, everything is owned by some Minister. That way, our class supports itself as well as the Commons, who on the extrasolar planets have to pay taxes. Here, a man can keep what he earns. Public works like the military forces are financed by industries owned in the name of the Technon.'

'But what do the Commoners do?'

'They have jobs – mostly in the cities, a few on the land. Some of them work for themselves, as artisans or meditechs or something similar. The Technon gives the orders on how to balance population and production, so that the economy runs a smooth course. Here, this ought to interest you.'

It was a museum. The general layout had not changed much, though there was a lot of unfamiliar gadgetry for better exhibition. Chanthavar led them to the historical-archeological section, the centuries around their own time. It was saddening how little had survived: a few coins, age-blurred in spite of electrolytic restoration; a chipped glass tumbler; a fragment of stone bearing the defaced name of some bank; the corroded remnant of a flintlock musket, found in the Sahara when it was being reclaimed; broken marble which had once been a statue. Chanthavar said that the Egyptian pyramids, part of the Sphinx, traces of buried cities, a couple of ruined dams in America and Russia, some hydrogen-bomb craters, were still around, otherwise nothing earlier than the Thirty-fifth Century. Time went on, relentlessly, and one by one the proud works of man were lost.

Langley found himself whistling, as if to keep up his courage. Chanthavar cocked an inquisitive head. 'What's that?'

'Conclusion to the Ninth Symphony – *Freude, schöne Götterfunken* – ever hear of it?'

'No.' There was a curious, wistful expression on the wide bony face. 'It's a shame. I rather like that.'

They had lunch at a terrace restaurant, where machines served a gaily dressed, stiff-mannered clientele of aristocrats. Chanthavar paid the bill with a shrug. 'I hate to put money into the purse of Minister Agaz – he's after my head – but you must admit he keeps a good chef.'

The guards did not eat; they were trained to a sparse diet and an untiring watchfulness.

'There's a lot to see, here in the upper levels,' said Chanthavar. He nodded at the discreet glow-sign of an amusement house. 'But it's more of the same. Come on downside for a change.'

A gravity shaft dropped them two thousand feet, and they stepped into another world.

Here there was no sun, no sky; walls and ceiling were metal, floors were soft and springy, and a ruler-straight drabness filled Langley's vision. The air was fresh enough, but it throbbed and rang with a noise that never ended – pumping, hammering, vibrating, the deep steady heartbeat of that

great machine which was the city. The corridors – streets –
were crowded, restless, alive with motion and shrill talking.

So these were the Commoners. Langley stood for a
moment in the shaft entrance, watching them. He didn't
know what he had expected – gray-clad zombies, perhaps –
but he was surprised. The disorderly mass reminded him of
cities he had seen in Asia.

Dress was a cheap version of the Ministerial: tunics for
men, long dresses for women; it seemed to fall into a
number of uniforms, green and blue and red, but was slopp-
ily worn. The men's heads were shaven; the faces reflected
that mixture of races which man on Earth had become;
there were incredible numbers of naked children playing
under the very feet of the mob; there was not that seg-
regation of the sexes which the upper levels enforced.

A booth jutting out from one wall was filled with cheap
pottery, and a woman carrying a baby in her arms haggled
with the owner. A husky, near-naked porter sweated under a
load of machine parts. Two young men squatted in the
middle of traffic, shooting dice. An old fellow sat dreamily
with a glass in his hand, just inside the door of a tavern. A
clumsy fist fight, watched by a few idlers, went on between a
man in red and one in green. An obvious streetwalker was
making up to a moronic-looking laborer. A slim, keen-faced
merchant – from Ganymede, Chanthavar said – was talking
quietly with a fat local buyer. A wealthy man rode a tiny
two-wheeler down the street, accompanied by two servants
who cleared a way for him. A jeweler sat in his booth, hammering on a bracelet. A three-year-old stumbled, sat down
hard, and broke into a wail which everybody ignored – it
could barely be heard through all the racket. An apprentice
followed his master, carrying a tool box. A drunk sprawled
happily against the wall. A vendor pushed a cart full of
steaming tidbits, crying his wares in a singsong older than
civilization. So much Langley could see, then it faded into
the general turbulence.

Chanthavar offered cigarettes, struck one for himself, and led the way behind a couple of guards. People fell aside, bowing respectfully and then resuming their affairs. 'We'll have to walk,' said the agent. 'No slideways down here.'

'What are the uniforms?' asked Blaustein.

'Different trades – metalworker, food producer, and so on. They have a guild system, highly organized, several years' apprenticeship, and there's a lot of rivalry between the guilds. As long as the Commons do their work and behave themselves, we leave them pretty much alone. The police – city-owned slaves – keep them in line if real trouble ever starts.' Chanthavar pointed to a burly-clad man in a steel helmet. 'It doesn't matter much what goes on here. They haven't the weapons or the education to threaten anything; such schooling as they get emphasizes how they must fit themselves to the basic system.'

'Who's that?' Matsumoto gestured to a man in form-fitting scarlet, his face masked, a knife in his belt, who slipped quietly between people indisposed to hinder him.

'Assassins' guild, though mostly they hire out to do burglaries and beatings. The Commoners aren't robots – we encourage free enterprise. They're not allowed firearms, so it's safe enough and keeps the others amused.'

'Divided, you mean,' said Langley.

Chanthavar spread his hands. 'What would you do? It isn't possible to have equality. It's been tried again and again in history, giving everybody a vote, and it's always failed – always, in a few generations, the worse politicians drove out the better. Because by definition, half the people always have below-average intelligence; and the average is not high. Nor can you let these mobs go just anywhere – Earth's too crowded.'

'It's a cultural matter,' said Langley. 'I know a lot of countries back around my own time started out with beautiful constitutions and soon fell into dictatorship: but that was because there was no background, no tradition. Some like Great Britain made it work for centuries, because they did have that kind of society, that ... common-sense attitude.'

'My friend, you can't make over a civilization,' said Chanthavar, 'and in reforming one, you have to use the materials available. The founders of the Technate knew that. It's too late; it was always too late. Look around you – think these apes are fit to decide public policy?' He sighed. 'Read your history and face it: war, poverty, and tyranny are the natural condition of man, the so-called golden ages are freak fluctations which soon collapse because they don't fit a creature only three hundred life-times out of the caves. Life is much too short to spend trying to alter the laws of nature. Ruthless use of strength is the law of nature.'

Langley gave up, became a tourist. He was interested in the factories, where men were ants scurrying around the metal titans they had built; in the schools, where a few years including hypnotic indoctrination were enough to teach the needed rudiments; in the dark, smoky, raucous taverns; in the homes, small crowded apartments with a moderate comfort, even stereoscopic shows of appropriate imbecility, and a rather cheerful, indulgent family life in a temple, where a crowd swaying and chanting its hymns to Father reminded him of an old-time camp meeting; in the little shops which lined the streets, last survival of handicraft and a surprisingly good folk art; in the market, which filled a gigantic open circle with shrilling women— Yes, a lot to see.

After dinner, which was at a spot patronized by the wealthier Common merchants, Chanthavar smiled. 'Near walked my legs off today,' he said. 'Now how about some fun? A city is known by its vices.'

'Well ... O.K.,' said Langley. He was a little drunk, the sharp pungent beer of the lower levels buzzed in his head. He didn't want women, not with memory still a bright pain

T–C

in him, but there ought to be games and— His purse was full
of bills and coins. 'Where to?'

'Dreamhouse, I think,' said Chanthavar, leading them
out. 'It's a favorite resort for all levels.'

The entrance was a cloudy blueness opening into many
small rooms. They took one, slipping life-masks over their
faces: living synthetic flesh which stung briefly as it connected to nerve endings in the skin and then was part of you.
'Everybody's equal here, everybody anonymous,' said
Chanthavar. 'Refreshing.'

'What is your wish, sirs?' The voice came from nowhere,
cool and somehow not human.

'General tour,' said Chanthavar. 'The usual. Here . . . put
a hundred solars in this slot, each of you. The place is expensive, but fun.'

They relaxed on what seemed a dry, fluffy cloud, and were
carried aloft. The guards formed an impassive huddle some
distance behind. Doors opened for them. They hung under a
perfumed sky of surrealistic stars and moons, looking down
on what appeared to be a deserted landscape not of Earth.

'Part illusion, part real,' said Chanthavar. 'You can have
any experience you can imagine here, for the right price.
Look—'

The cloud drifted through a rain which was blue and red
and golden fire, tingling as it licked over their bodies. Great
triumphant chords of music welled around them. Through
the whirling flames, Langley glimpsed girls of an impossible
loveliness, dancing on the air.

Then they were underwater, or so it seemed, with tropical
fish swimming through a green translucence, corals and
waving fronds underneath. Then they were in a red-lit
cavern, where the music was a hot pulse in the blood and
they shot at darting containers which landed to offer a drink
when hit. Then they were in a huge and jolly company of
people, singing and laughing and dancing and guzzling. A
pneumatic young female giggled and tugged at Langley's

arm – briefly, he wavered, there must be some drug in the air, then he said harshly: 'Scram!'

Whirled over a roaring waterfall, sporting through air which was somehow thick enough to swim in, gliding past grottoes and glens full of strange lights, and on into a gray swirling mist where you could not see a yard ahead. Here, in a dripping damp quiet which seemed to mask enormousness, they paused.

Chanthavar's shadowy form gestured, and there was a queer taut note in his muffled voice: 'Would you like to play Creator? Let me show you—' A ball of raging flame was in his hands, and from it he molded stars and strewed them through sightless immensity. 'Suns, planets, moons, people, civilization, and histories – you can make them here as you please.' Two stars crashed into each other. 'You can will yourself to see a world grow, any detail no matter how tiny, a million years in a minute or a minute stretched through a million years; you can smite it with thunder, and watch them cower and worship you.' The sun in Chanthavar's hands glowed dully through the fog. Tiny sparks which were planets flitted around it. 'Let me clear the mist, let there be light. Let there be Life and a History!'

Something moved in the wet smoky air. Langley saw a shadow striding between new-born constellations, a thousand light-years tall. A hand gripped his arm, and dimly he saw the pseudo-face beyond.

He writhed free, yelling, as the other hand sought his neck. A wire loop snaked out, tangling his ankles. There were two men now, closing in on him. Wildly, he groped backward. His fist connected with a cheek which bled artificial blood.

'*Chanthavar!*'

A blaster crashed, startlingly loud and brilliant. Langley hurled a giant red sun into one of the faces wavering near him. Twisting free of an arm about his waist, he kneed the vague form and heard a grunt of pain.

'Light!' bellowed Chanthavar. 'Get rid of this mist!'

The fog broke, slowly and raggedly. There was a deep clear blackness, the dark of outer vacuum, with stars swimming in it like fireflies. Then full illumination came on.

A man sprawled dead near Chanthavar, his stomach torn open by an energy bolt. The guards milled uneasily. Otherwise they were alone. The room was bare, coldly lit, Langley thought somewhere in his lurching mind that it was cruel to show the emptiness here where there had been dreams.

For a long moment, he and the agent stared at each other. Blaustein and Matsumoto were gone.

'Is . . . this . . . part of the fun?' asked Langley through his teeth.

'No.' A hunter's light flickered in Chanthavar's eyes. He laughed. 'Beautiful job! I'd like to have those fellows on my staff. Your friends have been stunned and kidnapped under my own eyes. Come on!'

CHAPTER SEVEN

THERE was a time of roaring confusion, as Chanthavar snapped orders into a visiphone, organizing a chase. Then he swung around to Langley. 'I'll have this warren searched, of course,' he said, 'but I don't imagine the kidnappers are still in it. The robots aren't set to notice who goes out in what condition, so that's no help. Nor do I expect to find the employee of this place who helped fix matters up for the snatch. But I've got the organization alerted, there'll be a major investigation hereabouts inside half an hour. And Brannoch's quarters are being watched already.'

'Brannoch?' repeated Langley stupidly. His brain felt

remote, like a stranger's, he couldn't throw off the air-borne drugs as fast as the agent.

'To be sure! Who else? Never thought he had this efficient a gang on Earth, but— They won't take your friends directly to him, of course, there'll be a hideout somewhere in the lower levels, not too much chance of finding it among fifteen million Commoners, but we'll try. We'll try!'

A policeman hurried up with a small, metal-cased object which Chanthavar took. 'Peel off that mask. This is an electronic scent-tracer, we'll try to follow the trail of the pseudo-faces – distinctive odor, so don't you confuse it. I don't think the kidnappers took the masks off in Dreamhouse, then someone might notice who they were carrying. Stick with us, we may need you. Let's go!'

A score of men, black-clad, armed, and silent, surrounded them. Chanthavar cast about the main exit. There was something of the questing hound over him – the aesthete, the hedonist, the casual philosopher, were blotted up in the hunter of men. A light glowed on the machine. 'A trail, all right,' he muttered. 'If only it doesn't get cold too fast— Damn it, why must they ventilate the lowers so well?' He set off at a rapid jog trot, his men keeping an easy pace. The milling crowds shrank away.

Langley was too bewildered to think. This was happening faster than he could follow, and the drugs of Dreamhouse were still in his blood, making the world unreal. Bob, Jim, now the great darkness had snatched them too, and would he ever see them again?

Why?

Down a drop-shaft, falling like autumn leaves, Chanthavar testing each exit as he passed it. The unceasing roar of machines grew louder, more frantic. Langley shook his head, trying to clear it, trying to master himself. It was like a dream, he was carried wildlessly along between phantoms in black, and—

He had to get away. He had to get off by himself, think in

peace; it was an obsession now, driving everything else out
of his head, he was in a nightmare and he wanted to wake
up. Sweat was clammy on his skin.

The light flashed, feebly. 'This way!' Chanthavar swung
out of a portal. 'Trail's weakening, but maybe—'

The guards pressed after him. Langley hung back,
dropped farther, and stepped out at the next level down.

It was an evil section, dim-lit and dingy, the streets almost
deserted. Closed doors lined the walls, litter blew about
under his feet, the stamping and grinding of machines filled
his universe. He walked fast, turning several corners, trying
to hide.

Slowly, his brain cleared. An old man in dirty garments
sat cross-legged beside a door, watching him out of filmy
eyes. A small group of grimed children played some game
under the white glare of a fluorolamp in the street ceiling. A
sleazy woman slunk close to him, flashing bad teeth in a
mechanical smile, and fell behind. A tall young man, ragged
and unshaven, leaned against the wall and followed his
movements with listless eyes. This was the slum, the oldest
section, poor and neglected, last refuge of failure; this was
where those whom the fierce life of the upper tiers had
broken fled, to drag out lives of no importance to the Technon. Under the noise of mills and furnaces, it was very
quiet.

Langley stopped, breathing hard. A furtive hand groped
from a narrow passage, feeling after the purse at his belt. He
slapped, and the child's bare feet pattered away into darkness.

Fool thing to do, he thought. *I could be murdered for my
cash. Let's find us a cop and get out of here, son.*

He walked on down the street. A legless beggar whined at
him, but he didn't dare show his money. New legs could
have been grown, but that was a costly thing. Well behind, a
tattered pair followed him. Where was a policeman? Didn't
anyone care what happened down here?

A huge shape came around a corner. It had four legs, a torso with arms, a nonhuman head. Langley hailed it. 'Which is the way out? Where's the nearest shaft going up? I'm lost.'

The alien looked blankly at him and went on. *No spikka da Inglees.* Etie Town, the section reserved for visitors of other races, was somewhere around here. That might be safe, though most of the compartments would be sealed off, their interiors poisonous to him. Langley went the way the stranger had come. His followers shortened the distance between.

Music thumped and wailed from an open door. There was a bar, a crowd, but not the sort where he could look for help. As the final drug-mists cleared, Langley realized that he might be in a very tight fix.

Two men stepped out of a passage. They were husky, well dressed for Commoners. One of them bowed. 'Can I do you a service, sir?'

Langley halted, feeling the coldness of his own sweat. 'Yes,' he said thickly. 'Yes, thanks. How do I get out of this section?'

'A stranger, sir?' They fell in, one on either side. 'We'll conduct you. Right this way.'

Too obliging! 'What are you doing down here?' snapped Langley.

'Just looking around, sir.'

The speech was too cultivated, too polite. *These aren't Commoners any more than I am!* 'Never mind. I . . . I don't want to bother you. Just point me right.'

'Oh, no, sir. That would be dangerous. This is not a good area to be alone in.' A large hand fell on his arm.

'No!' Langley stopped dead.

'We must insist, I'm afraid.' An expert shove, and he was being half dragged. 'You'll be all right, sir, just relax, no harm.'

The tall shape of a slave policeman hove into view.

Langley's breath rattled in his throat. 'Let me go,' he said. 'Let me go, or—'

Fingers closed on his neck, quite unobtrusively, but he gasped with the pain. When he had recovered himself, the policeman was out of sight again.

Numbly, he followed. The portal of a grav-shaft loomed before him. *They tracked me,* he thought bitterly. *Of course they did. I don't know how stupid a man can get, but I've been trying hard tonight. And the price of this stupidity is apt to be total!*

Three men appeared, almost out of nowhere. They wore the gray robes of the Society. 'Ah,' said one, 'you found him. Thank you.'

'What's this?' Langley's companions recoiled. 'Who're you? What d'you want?'

'We wish to see the good captain home,' answered one of the newcomers. His neatly bearded face smiled, a gun jumped into his hand.

'That's illegal . . . that weapon—'

'Possibly. But you'll be very dead if you don't— That's better. Just come with us, captain, if you please.'

Langley entered the shaft between his new captors. There didn't seem to be much choice.

CHAPTER EIGHT

THE strangers did not speak, but hurried him along. They seemed to know all the empty byways, their progress upwards was roundabout but fast and hardly another face was seen en route. Langley tried to relax, feeling himself swept along a dark and resistless tide.

Upper town again, shining pinnacles and loops of diamond light against the stars. The air was warm and sweet in his lungs, he wondered how much longer he would breathe it. Not far from the shaft exit, a massive octagonal tower reared out of the general complex, its architecture foreign to the slim soaring exuberance which was Technate work. A nimbus of radiance hung over its peak, with letters of flame running through it to spell out COMMERCIAL SOCIETY. Stepping onto a bridgeway, the four were borne up toward a flange near its middle.

As they got off onto the ledge, a small black aircraft landed noiselessly beside them. A voice came from it, amplified till it boomed through the humming quiet: 'Do not move farther. This is the police.'

Police! Langley's knees felt suddenly watery. He might have known – Chanthavar would not leave this place unwatched, he had sent an alarm when the spaceman was found missing, the organization was efficient, and now he was saved!

The three traders stood immobile, their faces like wood. A door dilated, and another man stepped from the building as five black-clad slaves and one Ministerial officer got out of the boat. It was Goltan Valti. He waited with the others, rubbing his hands together in a nervous washing motion.

The officer bowed slightly. 'Good evening, sir. I am pleased to see you have found the captain. You are to be commended.'

'Thank you, my lord,' bowed Valti. His voice was shrill, almost piping, and he blew out his fat cheeks and bobbed his shaggy head obsequiously. 'It is kind of you to come, but your assistance is not required.'

'We will take him home for you,' said the officer.

'Oh, sir, surely you will permit me to offer my poor hospitality to this unfortunate stranger. It is a firm rule of the Society, a guest may never leave without being treated.'

'I am sorry, sir, but he must.' In the vague, flickering light, the officer scowled, and there was a sharp ring in his tones. 'Later, perhaps. Now he must come with us. I have my orders.'

Valti bowed and scraped. 'I sympathize, sir, these dim eyes weep at the thought of conflict with your eminence, but poor and old and helpless worm though I be' – the whine faded into a buttery purr – 'nevertheless, I am forced to remind you, my lord, much against my will, which is only for pleasant relationships, that you are outside your jurisdiction. By the Treaty of Lunar, the Society has extra-territorial rights. Honored sir, I pray you not to force me into requesting your passport.'

The officer grew rigid. 'I told you I had my orders,' he said thinly.

The trader's bulky shape looked suddenly enormous against the sky. His beard bristled. But the voice remained light: 'Sir, my heart bleeds for you. But be so kind as to remember that this building is armed and armored. A dozen heavy guns are trained on you, and I must regretfully en-force the law. The captain will take refreshment with me. Afterward he shall be sent to his home, but at present it is most inhospitable to keep him standing in this damp air. Good evening, sir.' He took Langley's arm and walked him to the door. The other three followed, and the door closed behind them.

'I suppose,' said the spaceman slowly, 'that what I want isn't of much account.'

'I had not hoped to have the honor of talking with you privately so soon, captain,' answered Valti. 'Nor do I think you will regret a chat over a cup of good Ammonite wine. It gets a little bruised in transit, so delicate a palate as yours will detect that, but I humbly assert that it retains points of superiority.'

They had gone down a hall, and now a door opened for them. 'My study, captain,' bowed Valti. 'Please enter.'

It was a big, low-ceilinged, dim-lit room, lined with shelves which held not only microspools but some authentic folio volumes. The chairs were old and shabby and comfort· able, the desk was big and littered with papers, there was a haze of strong tobacco in the rather stuffy air. Langley's attention was drawn to a screen in which a stereoscopic figure was moving. Briefly, he failed to understand the words –

'Existence or nullity – thus the problem:
Whether more free-born mentally to endure
The blasts and bolts of adverse chance occurrence,
Or to shoot through a universe of troubles,
And counteracting, annul them?'

Then he realized. The actor had a queue; he wore a fur cap, a lacquered breastplate, and flowing black robes; he was reaching for a scimitar; the background was a kind of Grecian temple – but by all the gods, it was still Hamlet!

'An old folk play, I believe, captain,' said Valti, shuffling up behind him. 'They've been putting on some revivals lately – interesting material. I believe this is Martian of the Interregnum period.'

'No,' said Langley. 'A bit older than that.'

'Oh? From your own time, even? Very interesting!' Valti switched it off. 'Well, pray sit down and be comfortable. Here comes refreshment.'

A creature the size of a monkey, with a beaked face and strangely luminous eyes beneath small antennae, entered bearing a tray in skinny arms. Langley found a chair and accepted a cup of hot spiced wine and a plate of cakes. Valti wheezed and drank deep. 'Ah! That does these rheumatic old bones good. I fear medicine will never catch up with the human body, which finds the most ingenious new ways of getting deranged. But good wine, sir, good wine and a pretty girl and the dear bright hills of home, there is the best medicine that will ever be devised. Cigars, Thakt, if you please.'

The monkey-thing leaped grotesquely to the desk and extended a box. Both men took one, and Langley found his good. The alien sat on Valti's shoulder, scratching its own green fur and giggling. Its eyes never left the spaceman.

'Well—' After the last couple of hours, Langley felt exhausted. There was no more fight in him, he relaxed and let the weariness run through nerve and muscle. But his head seemed abnormally clear. 'Well, Mr. Valti, what was all this foofaraw about?'

The trader blew smoke and sat back, crossing his stumpy legs. 'Events are beginning to move with uncomfortable rapidity,' he said in a quiet tone. 'I'm glad this chance came to see you.'

'Those cops seemed anxious that I shouldn't.'

'Of course.' The deep-sunken little eyes twinkled. 'But it will take them some time to line up those collections of reflexes they call brains and decide to attack me; by then, you will be home, for I shall not detain you long. The good Chanthavar, now, would not stall, but he is fortunately engaged elsewhere.'

'Yes . . . trying to find my friends.' Langley felt a dull grief in him. 'Do you know they were taken?'

'I do.' There was sympathy in the tone. 'I have my own agents in the Solar forces, and know more or less all which happened tonight.'

'Then – where are they? How are they?'

Bleakness twisted the half-hidden mouth. 'I am very much afraid for them. They are probably in the power of Lord Brannoch. They may be released, I don't know, but—' Valti sighed. 'I've no spies in his organization, nor he in mine . . . I hope; both of them are too small, too uncorrupted, too well set up – unlike Sol's. We must be very much in the dark with regard to each other.'

'Are you sure, then, that it was he who—'

'Who else? Chanthavar had no need that I can see to stage such an affair, he could order all of you arrested any time he chose. None of the other foreign states are in this at all, they are too weak. Brannoch is known to head Centaurian military intelligence at Sol, though so far he has been clever enough to leave no evidence which would be grounds for his expulsion. No, the only powers which count in this part of the galaxy are Sol, Centauri, and the Society.'

'And why,' asked Langley slowly, 'would Brannoch take them?'

'Isn't it obvious? The alien, Saris Hronna I think he's called. They may know where to find him.

'You don't realize what a fever he has thrown all of us into. You have been watched every minute by agents of all three powers. I toyed with the idea of having you snatched myself, but the Society is too peaceful to be very good at that sort of thing, and Brannoch beat us to it. The moment I learned what had happened, I sent a hundred men out to try to locate you. Fortunately, one group succeeded.'

'They almost didn't,' said Langley. 'They had to take me away from two others – Centaurians, I suppose.'

'Of course. Well ... I don't think Brannoch will try to assault this stronghold, especially since he will have hopes of getting the information from your friends. Do you think he will?'

'Depends.' Langley narrowed his eyes and took a long drag of smoke. 'I doubt it, though. They never got very intimate with Saris. I did – we used to talk for hours – though I still can't claim to know just what makes him tick.'

'Ah, so.' Valti took a noisy sip of wine. There was no expression in the heavy face. 'Do you know why he is so important?'

'I think so. Military value of his ability to damp out or control electronic currents and so forth. But I'm surprised you haven't got a machine to do the same thing.'

'Science died long ago,' said Valti. 'I, who have seen worlds where they are still progressing, though behind us as yet, know the difference between a living science and a dead one. The spirit of open-minded inquiry became extinct in known human civilizations quite a while back: the rigidity of social forms, together with the fact that research no longer discovered anything not predicted by theory, caused that. It was, after all, reasonable to assume that the variety of natural laws was finite, that a limit had been reached. Nowadays, the very desire to inquire further is lacking. Sol is stagnant, the other systems barbaric under their façade of machine technology, the Society too loosely organized to support a scientific community. A dead end, yes, yes, so it goes.'

Langley tried to concentrate on abstractions, to escape the new fear which gnawed in his breast. 'And so now something turns up which is *not* accounted for by standard theory. And everybody wants to study it and learn about it and duplicate it on a grand scale for military purposes. Yeah. I get the idea.'

Valti looked at him under drooping lids. 'There are, of course, ways to make a man talk,' he said. 'Not torture – nothing so crude – but drugs which unlock the tongue. Chanthavar has hesitated to use them on you, because if you do not, after all, have an idea where Saris is, the rather unpleasant process could easily set up a subconscious bloc which would forbid you to think further about the problem. However, he may now be desperate enough to do so. He will surely do it the moment he suspects you have deduced something. Have you?'

'Why should I tell you?'

Valti looked patient. 'Because only the Society can be trusted with a decisive weapon.'

'Only one party can,' said Langley dryly, 'but which party depends on who you're talking to. I've heard that song before.'

'Consider,' said Valti. His voice remained dispassionate. 'Sol is a petrified civilization, interested only in maintaining the *status quo*. The Centaurians brag a great deal about frontier vigor, but they are every bit as dead between the ears; if they won, there would be an orgy of destruction followed by a pattern much the same, nothing new except a change of masters. If either system suspects that the other has gotten Saris, it will attack at once, setting off the most destructive war in a history which has already seen destruction on a scale you cannot imagine. The other, smaller, states are no better, even if they were in a position to use the weapon effectively.'

'I don't know,' said Langley. 'What people seem to need today is a good swift kick in the pants. Maybe Centauri can give it to them.'

'Not with any beneficial effect. What is Centauri? A triple-star system. Alpha A has two habitable planets, Thor and Freyja. Alpha B has two semi-poisonous ones slowly being made habitable. Proxima is a dim red dwarf with one inhabited planet, the frigid giant Thrym. Otherwise there are only mining colonies maintained with great difficulty. The Thorians conquered and assimilated the men of the other worlds long ago. They established contact with the Thrymans, showed them modern technology; soon the natives – already highly civilized – were equal to their teachers. Then Thrym denied them right to settle the Proximan System. A war was fought over it, which ended officially in compromise and unification; actually, Thrym had the upper hand, and its representatives occupy key positions in the League. Brannoch has Thryman advisors here on Earth, and I wonder who is really the chief.

'I've no prejudice against nonhumans, but Thrym makes me feel cold. They're too remote from man, I think they have little use for him except as a tool toward some purpose of their own. Study the situation, study history, and I think you'll agree. A Centaurian conquest, quite apart from the killing of some billions of innocent people, would not be an infusion of invigorating barbarian blood. It would be a move in a very old and very large chess game.'

'All right.' Langley gave up. 'Maybe you're right. But what claim has your precious Society got? Who says you're a race of—' He paused, realized that there was no word for saint or angel, and finished weakly: 'Why do you deserve anything?'

'We are not interested in imperialism,' said Valti. 'We carry on trade between the stars—'

'Probably cleaning the pants off both ends.'

'Well, an honest businessman has to live. But we have no planet, we are not interested in having one, our home is space itself. We do not kill except in self-defense; normally we avoid a fight by simply retreating, there is always plenty of room in the universe and a long jump makes it easy to overcome your enemies by merely outliving them. We are a people to ourselves, with our own history, traditions, laws – the only humane and neutral power in the known galaxy.'

'Tell me more,' said Langley. 'So far I've only got your word. You must have some central government, someone to make decisions and coordinate you. Who are they? Where are they?'

'I will be perfectly honest, captain,' said Valti in a soft tone. 'I do not know.'

'Eh?'

'No one knows. Each ship is competent to handle ordinary affairs for itself. We file reports at the planetary offices, pay our tax – where the reports and the money go, I don't know, nor do the groundlings in the offices. There is a chain of communications, a cell-type secret bureaucracy which would be impossible to trace through tens of light-years. I rank high, running the Solar offices at present, and can make many decisions for myself, but I get special orders now and then through a sealed circuit. There must be at least one of the chiefs here on Earth, but where and who – or what – I couldn't say.'

'How does this . . . government . . . keep you in line?'

'We obey,' said Valti. 'Ship discipline is potent, even on those who like myself are recruited from planets rather than born in space. The rituals, the oaths – conditioning, if you will – I know of no case where an order has been deliberately violated. But we are a free people, there is no slavery and no aristocracy among us.'

'Except for your bosses,' murmured Langley. 'How do you know they're working for your own good?'

'You needn't read any sinister or melodramatic implications into a security policy, captain. If the headquarters and identity of our chiefs were known, they would be all too liable to attack and annihilation. As it is, promotion to the bureaucracy involves complete disappearance, probably surgical disguise; I will gladly accept the offer if it is ever made to me.

'Under its bosses, as you call them, the Society has prospered in the thousand years since its founding. We are a force to be reckoned with. You saw how I was able to make that police officer knuckle under.'

Valti took a deep breath and plunged into business. 'I have not, as yet, received any command about Saris. If I had been told to keep you prisoner, be sure you would not leave here. But as things are, I still have considerable latitude.

'Here is my offer. There are small interplanetary flitters hidden here and there on Earth. You can leave anytime. Away from Earth, safely concealed by sheer volume of space unless you know her orbit, is an armed light-speed cruiser. If you will help me find Saris, I will take you two away, and do what I can to rescue your companions. Saris will be studied, but he will not be harmed in any manner, and if he wishes can later be returned to his home world. You can join the Society, or you can be set up on some human-colonized planet beyond the region known to Sol and Centauri. There are many lovely worlds out there, a wide cultural variety, places where you can feel at home again. Your monetary reward will give you a good start.

'I do not think you will like Earth any more, captain. Nor do I think you will like the responsibility of unleashing a war which will devastate planets. I believe your best course is with us.'

Langley stared at the floor. Weariness was close to overwhelming him. To go home, to creep down light-years and centuries until he found Peggy again, it was a scream within him.

But—

'I don't know,' he mumbled. 'How can I tell if you're not lying?' With an instinct of self-preservation: 'I don't know where Saris is either, you realize. Doubt if I can find him myself.'

Valti lifted a skeptical brow, but said nothing.

'I need time to think,' pleaded Langley. 'Let me sleep on it.'

'If you wish.' Valti got up and rummaged in a drawer. 'But remember, Chanthavar or Brannoch may soon remove all choice from you. Your decision, if it is to be your own, must be made soon.'

He took out a small, flat plastic box and handed it over. 'This is a communicator, keyed to a frequency which varies continuously according to a random-chosen series. It can only be detected by a similarly tuned instrument which I possess. If you want me, press this button and call; it need not be held to your mouth. I may even be able to rescue you from armed force, though it's best to be quiet about this affair. Here . . . keep it next to your skin, under your clothes, it will hang on of itself and is transparent to ordinary spy-beams.'

Langley rose. 'Thanks,' he muttered. 'Decent of you to let me go.' *Or is it only a trick to disarm me?*

'It's nothing, captain.' Valti waddled ahead of him to the

outside flange. An armored police craft hovered just beyond
its edge. 'I believe transportation home is waiting for you.
Good night, sir.'

'Good night,' said Langley.

CHAPTER NINE

WEATHER CONTROL had decreed rain for this area today, and
Lora stood under a low gray sky with her highest towers
piercing its mists. Looking out of the window which made
one wall of his living room, Brannoch saw only a wet metal
gleam, fading into the downward rush of rain. Now and then
lightning flickered, and when he told the window to open
there was a cool damp breeze on his face.

He felt caged. As he paced the room, up and down and
around, there was rage in his heart, and he snapped his
report as if every word had to be bitten off and spat out.

'Nothing,' he said. 'Not one damned sterile thing. They
didn't know. They had no idea where the creature might be.
Their memories were probed down to the cellular level, and
nothing turned up we could use.'

'Has Chanthavar any clue?' asked the flat mechanical
voice.

'No. My Mesko agent's last report said that a warehouse
was broken into the night that flier was stolen, and several
cases of space rations removed. So all the being had to do
was hide these in whatever den he's got, release the flier on
automatic, and settle down to wait. Which he's apparently
been doing ever since.'

'It would be strange if human food would sustain him
indefinitely,' said Thrymka. 'The probabilities all favor his
dietary requirements being at least slightly different from

yours – there will be some small cumulative deficiency or poisoning. Eventually he will sicken and die.'

'That may take weeks,' snarled Brannoch, 'and meanwhile he may find some way of getting what he needs – it may only be some trace element, titanium or – anything. Or he may make a deal with one of the parties looking for him. I tell you, there's no time to lose!'

'We are well aware of that,' answered Thrymka. 'Have you punished your agents for their failure to get Langley too?'

'No. They tried, but luck was against them. They almost had him, down in the Old City, but then armed members of the Society took him away. Could he have been bribed by Valti? It might be a good idea to knock that fat slug off.'

'No.'

'But—'

'No. Council policy forbids murder of a Society member.'

Brannoch shrugged bitterly. 'For fear they'll stop trading with Centauri? We should be building our own merchant ships. We should be independent of everybody. There'll come a day when the Council will see—'

'After you have founded a new dynasty to rule over a Centaurian interstellar hegemony? Perhaps!' There was the faintest lilt of sardonicism in the artificial voice. 'But continue your report; you know we prefer verbal communication. Did not Blaustein and Matsumoto have any useful information at all?'

'Well ... yes. They said that if anyone could predict where Saris is and what he'll do, it's Langley. Just our luck that he was the one man we did not succeed in grabbing. Now Chanthavar has mounted such a guard over him that it'd be impossible.' Brannoch ran a hand through his yellow mane. 'I've put an equal number of my men to watching him, of course. They'd at least make it difficult for Chanthavar to spirit him away. For the time being, it's a deadlock.'

'What disposition has been made of the two prisoners?'

'Why ... they're still in the Old City hideout. Anesthetized. I thought I'd have memory of the incident wiped from them, and let them go. They're not important.'

'They may be,' said the monster – or the monsters. 'If returned to Chanthavar, they will be two hostages by which he may be able to compel Langley's cooperation: which is something we cannot do without showing our hands too much, probably getting ourselves deported. But it is dangerous and troublesome for us to keep them. Have them killed and the bodies disintegrated.'

Brannoch stopped dead. After a long time, during which the beat of rain against the window seemed very loud, he shook his head. 'No.'

'Why not?'

'Assassination in the line of business is one thing. But we don't kill helpless prisoners on Thor.'

'Your reason is logically insufficient. Give the orders.'

Brannoch stood quiet. The concealing wall pattern swirled slowly before his eyes; opposite it, rain was liquid silver running down the single big pane.

It struck him suddenly that he had never seen a Thryman. There were stereographs, but under the monstrous weight of their atmosphere, dragged down by a planet of fifty thousand miles diameter and three Earth gravities, no man could live. Theirs was a world in which ice was like rock to form mountains, where rivers and seas of liquid ammonia raged through storms which could swallow Earth whole, where life based its chemistry on hydrogen and ammonia instead of oxygen and water, where explosions of gas burned red through darkness, where the population of the dominant species was estimated at fifty billions and a million years of recorded history had united them in one unhuman civilization – it was not a world for men, and he wished sometimes that men had never sent robots down to contact the

Thrymans, never traded instruction in the modern science which alone was able to maintain vacuum tubes against that pressure, for their chemicals.

He considered what was going on inside that tank. Four thick disks, six feet in diameter, slaty blue, each stood on six short legs with wide, clawed feet; between each pair of legs was an arm ending in a three-fingered hand of fantastic strength. A bulge in the center of the disk was the head, rigidly fixed, with four eyes arranged around a trunklike feeler on top and tympana for ears; underneath was the mouth and another trunk which was nose and feeder. You could not tell one from another, not by appearance or acts. It made no difference whether Thrymka-1 or Thrymka-2 spoke.

'You are debating whether or not to refuse,' said the microphonic voice. 'You are not especially fond of us.'

That was the damnable part of it. At short range, a Thryman could read your mind, you could have no thought and make no plan which he didn't know. It was one reason why they were valuable advisors. The other reason was tied in with the first: by joining feelers, they could discard spoken language, communicate directly by thought – nerve to nerve, a linkage in which individuality was lost and several intelligent, highly specialized entities became one brain of unimaginable power. The advice of such multi-brains had done much to give the League of Alpha Centauri its present strength.

But they weren't human. They weren't remotely human, they had almost nothing in common with man. They traded within the League, a swapping of mutually unavailable materials; they sat on the Council, held high executive positions – but the hookup ability made their minds quasi-immortal and altogether alien. Nothing was known of their culture, their art, their ambitions; whatever emotions they had were so foreign that the only possible communication with humankind was on the level of cold logic.

And, curse it all, a man was more than a logic machine.

'Your thinking is muddy,' said Thrymka. 'You may clarify it by formulating your objections verbally.'

'I won't have those men murdered,' said Brannoch flatly. 'It's an ethical question. I'd never forget what I had done.'

'Your society has conditioned you along arbitrary lines,' said Thrymka. 'Like most of your relationship-concepts, it is senseless, contra-survival. Within a unified civilization, which man does not possess, such an ethic could be justified, but not in the face of existing conditions. You are ordered to have those men killed.'

'Suppose I don't?' asked Brannoch softly.

'When the Council hears of your insubordination, you will be removed and all your chances for attaining your own ambitions vanish.'

'The Council needn't hear. I could crack that tank of yours. You'd explode like deep-sea fish. A very sad accident.'

'You will not do that. You cannot dispense with us. Also, the fact of your guilt would be known to all Thrymans on the Council as soon as you appeared before it.'

Brannoch's shoulders slumped. They had him, and they knew it. According to his own orders from home, they had the final say – always.

He poured himself a stiff drink and gulped it down. Then he thumbed a special communicator. 'Yantri speaking. Get rid of those two motors. Dismantle the parts. Immediately. That's all.'

The rain poured in an endless heavy stream. Brannoch stared emptily out into it. Well – that was that. *I tried.*

The glow of alcohol warmed him. It had gone against the grain, but he had killed many men before, no few of them with his own hand. Did the manner of their death make such a difference? There were larger issues at stake. There was his own nation, a proud folk, should they become the tributaries of this walking corpse which was Solar civilization? Two lives against a whole culture?

And there was the land. Always there was the land, space and fertility, a place to strike roots, a place to build homes and raise sons. There was something unreal about a city. Money was a fever-dream, a will-o'-the-wisp which had exhausted many lives. Only in soil was there strength.

And Earth had fair broad acres.

He shook himself, driving out the last cold which lay in his blood. Much to do yet. 'I suppose,' he said, 'that you know Langley is coming here today.'

'We have read that much in your brain. We are not sure why Chanthavar permits it.'

'To get a lead on me, of course, an idea of my procedures. Also, he would have to set himself against higher authorities, some of whom are in my pay, who have decreed that Langley shall have maximum freedom for the time being. There's a good deal of sentimentality about this man from the past and— Well, Chanthavar would defy them if he thought there was something to gain; but right now he wants to use Langley as bait for me. Give me enough voltage to electrocute myself.'

Brannoch grinned, suddenly feeling almost cheerful. 'And I'll play along. I've no objections at all to his knowing my game at present, because there isn't much he can do about it. I've invited Langley to drop over for a talk. If he knows where Saris is, you can read it in his mind: I'll direct the conversation that way. If he doesn't, then I have a scheme for finding out exactly when he's figured out the problem and what the answer is.'

'The balance is very delicate,' said Thrymka. 'The moment Chanthavar suspects we have a lead, he will take measures.'

'I know. But I'm going to activate the whole organization – spying, sabotage, sedition, all over the Solar System. That will keep him busy, make him postpone his arrest and interrogation of Langley till he's sure the fellow knows. Meanwhile, we can—' A bell chimed. 'That must be him now, downshaft. Here we go!'

Langley entered with a slow step, hesitating in the doorway. He looked very tired. His conventional clothes were no disguise for him – even if he had not been of fairly unmixed race, you would have known him for an outsider by his gait, his gestures, a thousand subtle hints. Brannoch thought in a mood of sympathy how lonesome the man must be. Then, with a secret laughter: *We'll fix that!*

Stepping forward, his flame-red cloak swirling from his shoulders, the Centaurian smiled. 'Good day, captain. It's very kind of you to come. I've been looking forward to a talk with you.'

'I can't stay long,' said Langley.

Brannoch flashed a glance at the window. A fighting ship hovered just outside, rain sluicing off its flanks. There would be men posted everywhere, spy-beams, weapons in readiness. No use to try kidnapping this time. 'Well, please sit down. Have a drink.' Flopping his own huge form into a chair: 'You're probably bored with silly questions about your period and how you like it here, I won't bother you that way. But I did want to ask you something about the planets you stopped at.'

Langley's gaunt face tightened. 'Look here,' he said slowly, 'the only reason I came was to try and get my friends away from you.'

Brannoch shrugged. 'I'm very sorry about that.' His tone was gentle. 'But you see, I haven't got them. I'll admit I wanted to, but somebody else got there first.'

'If that isn't a lie, it'll do till one comes along,' said the spaceman coldly.

Brannoch sipped his drink. 'Look here, I can't prove it to you. I don't blame you for being suspicious. But why fasten the guilt on me particularly? There are others who were just as anxious. The Commercial Society, for instance.'

'They—' Langley hesitated.

'I know. They picked you up a couple nights ago. News gets around. They must have sweet-talked you. How do you know they were telling the truth? Goltam Valti likes the devious approach. He likes to think of himself as a web-weaver, and he's not bad at it either.'

Langley fixed him with tormented eyes. 'Did you or did you not take those men?' he asked harshly.

'On my honor, I did not.' Brannoch had no scruples when it came to diplomacy. 'I had nothing to do with what happened that night.'

'There were two groups involved. One was the Society. What was the other?'

'Possibly Valti's agents, too. It'd be helpful if you thought of him as a rescuer. Or . . . here's a possibility. Chanthavar himself staged that kidnaping. He wanted to try interrogation but keep you in reserve. When you escaped him, Valti's gang may have seized the chance. Or Valti himself may be in Chanthavar's pay – or even, fantastic as it sounds, Chanthavar in Valti's. The permutations of bribery—' Brannoch smiled. 'I imagine you got a good scolding when you returned to friend Channy.'

'Yeah. I told him what to do with it, too. I've been pushed around long enough.' Langley took a deep gulp of his drink.

'I'm looking into the affair,' said Brannoch. 'I have to know myself. So far, I've not been able to discover anything. It is not that there are no clues – but too many.'

Langley's fingers twisted together. 'Think I'll ever see those boys again?' he asked.

'It's hard to say. But don't set your hopes up, and don't accept any offers to trade their lives for your information.'

'I won't . . . or wouldn't have . . . I think. There's too much at stake.'

'No,' murmured Brannoch. 'I don't think you would.'

He relaxed still further and drawled out the key question: '*Do* you know where Saris Hronna is?'

'No, I don't.'

'Haven't you any ideas? Isn't there some probable place?'

'I don't know.'

'You may be stalling, of course,' said Brannoch. 'I won't badger you about it. Just remember, I'm prepared to offer a very generous payment, protection, and transportation to the world of your choice, in return for that information. The world may well be Earth herself . . . in a few years.'

'So you do plan to attack her?'

Damn the fellow! Mind like a bulldog. Brannoch smiled easily. 'You've heard about us from our enemies,' he said. 'I'll admit we aren't a sweet-tempered people. We're farmers, fishermen, miners, mechanics, the noble isn't very much different from the smallholder except in owning more land. Why don't you get a book about us from the library, strain out the propaganda, and see for yourself?

'Ever since we got our independence, Sol has been trying to retake us. The Technon's idea is that only a unified civilization – under itself – should exist; everything else is too risky. Our notion is that all the cultures which have grown up have a right to their own ways of life, and to blazes with the risks. You can't unify man without destroying the variety and color which makes him worth having around – at least, you can't unify him under anything as deadening as a machine which does all his thinking for him.

'Sol is a menace to our self-respect. She's welcome to sit back and let her own arteries harden, but we don't want any part of it. When she tries to force it on us, we have to resist. Eventually, it probably will be necessary to destroy the Technon and occupy this system. Frankly, I don't think much will be lost. We could make those sheep down in

low-level back into human beings. We don't *want* to fight—
Father knows there's enough to do in our own system – but
it looks as if we'll have to.'

'I've heard all the arguments before,' said Langley. 'They
were current back around my own time. Too bad they
haven't been settled yet, despite all the centuries.'

'They never will be. Man is just naturally a rebel, a
diversifier; there'll always be nonconformists and those
who'd force conformity. You must admit, captain, that
some of these eternal arguments are better than others.'

'I . . . suppose so.'. Langley glanced up. 'I can't help you
anyway. Saris' hangout isn't known to me either.'

'Well, I promised I wouldn't pester you. Relax, captain.
You look like outworn applesauce. Have another drink.'

The talk strayed for an hour, wandering over stars and
planets. Brannoch exerted himself to charm, and thought he
was succeeding.

'I've got to go,' said Langley at last. 'My nursemaids must
be getting fretful.'

'As you say. Come in again any time.' Brannoch saw him
to the door. 'Oh, by the way. There'll be a present for you
when you get back. I think you'll like it.'

'Huh?' Langley stared at him.

'Not a bribe. No obligation. If you don't keep it, I won't
be offended. But it occurred to me that all the people trying
to use you as a tool never stopped to think that you are a
man.' Brannoch clapped his shoulder. 'So long. Good
luck.'

When he was gone, the Thorian whirled back toward his
listeners. There was a flame in him. 'Did you get it?' he
snapped. 'Did you catch any thoughts?'

There was a pause. Chanthavar didn't know, thought
Brannoch half drunkenly, or he would never have let Langley come here. Even the Thorians hadn't realized for a long
time that a Thryman was telepathic, and since discovering it

they had been careful to keep the fact secret. Maybe ...
maybe—

'No,' said the voice. 'We could not read his mind at all.'

'*What?*'

'It was gibberish. There was nothing recognizable. Now
we must depend on your scheme.'

Brannoch slumped into a chair. Briefly, he felt dismayed.
Why? Had a slow accumulation of mutations altered the
human brain that much? He didn't know; the Thrymans
had never told anyone how their telepathy worked.

But— Well, Langley was still a man. There was still a
chance. A very good chance, if I know men. Brannoch
sighed gustily and tried to ease the tautness within himself.

CHAPTER TEN

THE police escort dogged him all the way back. And there
would be others in the throngs on the bridgeways, hidden
behind the blurring rain which runneled off the transparent
coverings. No more peace, no more privacy. Unless he gave
in, told what he really thought.

He'd have to, or before long his mind would be wrenched
open and its knowledge pried out. So far, reflected Langley,
he'd done a good job of dissimulation, of acting baffled. It
wasn't too hard. He came from another civilization, and his
nuances of tone and gesture and voice could not be interpreted by the most skilled psychologist today. Also, he'd
always been a good poker player.

But who? Chanthavar, Brannoch, Valti – didn't Saris
have any rights in the matter? They could all have been

lying to him, there might not be a word of truth in any of their arguments. Maybe no one should have the new power, maybe it was best to burn Saris to ash with an energy beam and forget him. But how could even that be done?

Langley shook his head. He had to decide, and fast. If he read a few of those oddly difficult books, learned something – just a little, just enough for a guess as to who could most be trusted. Or maybe he should cut cards. It wouldn't be any more senseless than the blind blundering fate which seemed to rule human destiny.

No ... he had to live with himself, all the rest of his days.

He came out on the flange of the palace tower which held his apartment. (Only his. It was very big and lonely now, without Jim and Bob.) The hall bore him to a shaft, and he sped upward toward his own level. Four guards, unhuman-looking in the stiff black fabric of combat armor, followed; but at least they'd stay outside his door.

Langley stopped to let it scan him. 'Open, sesame,' he said in a tired voice, and walked through. It closed behind him.

Then, for a little while, there was an explosion in his head, and he stood in a stinging darkness.

It lifted. He swayed on his feet, not moving, feeling the tears that ran down his face. 'Peggy,' he whispered.

She came toward him with the same long-legged, awkward grace he remembered. The plain white dress was belted to a slender waist, and ruddy hair fell to her shoulders. The eyes were big and green, there was gentleness on the wide mouth, her nose was tilted and there was a dusting of freckles across its bridge. When she was close, she stopped and bent the knee to him. He saw how the light slid over her burnished hair.

He reached out as if to touch her, but his hand wouldn't go all the way. Suddenly his teeth were clapping in his jaws, and there was a chill in his flesh. Blindly, he turned from her.

He beat his fists against the wall, hardly touching it, letting the forces that shuddered within him expend themselves in controlling muscles that wanted to batter down a world. It seemed like forever before he could face her again. She was still waiting.

'You're not Peggy,' he said through his tears. 'It isn't you.'

She did not understand the English, but must have caught his meaning. The voice was low, as Hers had been, but not quite the same. 'Sir, I am called Marin. I was sent as a gift by the Lord Brannoch dhu Crombar. It will be my pleasure to serve you.'

At least, thought Langley, *Brannoch had enough brains to give her another name.*

His heart, racing in its cage of ribs, began skipping beats, and he snapped after air. Slowly, he fumbled over to the service robot. 'Give me a sedative,' he said. 'I want to remain conscious but calm.' The voice was strange in his ears.

When he had gulped the liquid down, he felt a darkness rising. His hands tingled as warmth returned. The heart slowed, the lungs expanded, the sweating skin shivered and eased. There was a balance within him, as if his grief had aged many years.

He studied the girl, and she gave him a timid smile. No – not Peggy. The face and figure, yes, but no American woman had ever smiled in just that way, that particular curve of lips; she was a little taller, he saw, and did not walk like one born free, and the voice—

'Where did you come from?' he asked, vaguely amazed at the levelness in his tone. 'Tell me about yourself.'

'I am a Class Eight slave, sir,' she answered, meekly but with no self-consciousness about it. 'We are bred for intelligent, pleasant companionship. My age is twenty. The Lord Brannoch purchased me a few days ago, had surgical alterations and psychological conditioning performed, and sent me here as a gift to you. I am yours to command, sir.'

'Anything goes, eh?'

'Yes, sir.' There was a small flicker of fear in her eyes, stories about perverted and sadistic owners must have run through the breeding and training centers; but he liked the game way she faced up to him.

'Never mind,' he said. 'You've nothing to worry about. You're to go back to the Lord Brannoch and tell him that he's just wrecked any chance he ever had of getting my coöperation.'

She flushed, and her eyes filmed with tears. At least she had pride – well, of course Brannoch would have known Langley wasn't interested in a spiritless doll — It must have been an effort to control her reply: 'Then you don't want me, sir?'

'Only to deliver that message. Get out.'

She bowed and turned to go. Langley leaned against the wall, his fists knotted together. *O Peggy, Peggy!*

'Just a minute!' It was as if someone else had spoken. She stopped.

'Yes, sir?'

'Tell me . . . what'll happen to you now?'

'I don't know, sir. The Lord Brannoch may punish—' She shook her head with a queer, stubborn honesty that did not fit a slave. But Peggy had been that way, too. 'No, sir. He will realize I am not to blame. He may keep me for a while, or sell me to someone else. I don't know.'

Langley felt a thickness in his throat.

'No.' He smiled, it hurt his mouth. 'I'm sorry. You . . . startled me. Don't go away. Sit down.'

He found a chair for himself, and she curled slim legs beneath her to sit at his feet. He touched her head with great gentleness. 'Do you know who I am?' he asked.

'Yes, sir. Lord Brannoch said you were a spaceman from very long ago who got lost and – I look like your wife, now.

I suppose he used pictures to make the copy. He said he thought you'd like to have someone who looked like her.'

'And what else? What were you supposed to do? Talk me into helping him? He wants my help in an important matter.'

'No, sir.' She met his eyes steadily. 'I was only to obey your wishes. It—' A tiny frown creased her brow, so much like Peggy's that Langley felt his heart crack within him. 'It may be he was relying on your gratitude.'

'Fat chance!' Langley tried to think. It wasn't like Brannoch, who must be a cynical realist, to assume that this would make the spaceman come slobbering to him. Or was it? Some traits of human nature had changed with the change in all society. Maybe a present-day Earthman would react like that.

'Do you expect me to feel obligated to him?' he asked slowly.

'No, sir. Why should you? I'm not a very expensive gift.'

Langley wished for his old pipe. He'd have to have some tobacco cut for it special one of these days, he thought vaguely; nobody smoked pipes any more. He stroked her bronze hair with a hand which the drug had again made steady.

'Tell me something about yourself, Marin,' he said. 'What sort of life did you lead?'

She described it, competently, without resentment and not without humor. The center didn't meet any of Langley's preconceived notions; far from being a hole of lust, it sounded like a rather easy-going institution. There had been woods and fields to stroll in between the walls, there had been an excellent education, there had been no attempt – except for conditioning to acceptance of being property – to prevent each personality from growing its own way. But of course, those girls were meant for high-class concubines.

T–D

With the detachment lent him by the sedative, Langley perceived that Marin could be very useful to him. He asked her a few questions about history and current events, and she gave him intelligent answers. Maybe her knowledge could help him decide what to do.

'Marin,' he asked dreamily, 'have you ever ridden a horse?'

'No, sir. I can pilot a car or flier, but I was never on an animal. It would be fun to try.' She smiled, completely at ease now.

'Look,' he said, 'drop that superior pronoun and stop calling me "sir". My name's Edward – plain Ed.'

'Yes, sir ... Edwy.' She frowned with a childlike seriousness. 'I'll try to remember. Excuse me if I forget. And in public, it would be better to stay by the usual rules.'

'O.K. Now—' Langley couldn't face the clear eyes, he stared out at the rain instead. 'Would you like to be free?'

'Sir?'

'Ed! I suppose I can manumit you. Wouldn't you like to be a free agent?'

'It's ... very kind of you,' she replied slowly. 'But—'

'Well?'

'But what could I do? I'd have to go to low-level, become a Commoner's wife or a servant or a prostitute. There isn't any other choice.'

'Nice system. Up here, you're at least protected, and among your intellectual equals. O.K., it was just a thought. Consider yourself part of the furniture.'

She chuckled. 'You're ... nice,' she said. 'I was very lucky.'

'Like hell you were. Look, I'm going to keep you around because I haven't the heart to turn you out. But there may well be danger. I'm right in the middle of an interstellar poker game and – I'll try to get you out from under if things go sour, but I may not be able to. Tell me honestly, can you face the prospect of getting killed or ... or anything?'

'Yes, Edwy. That is of the essence of my training. We cannot know our future – so we must learn the courage to accept it.'

'I wish you wouldn't talk that way,' he said gloomily. 'But I suppose you can't help it. People may still be the same underneath, but they think different on top. Well—'

'What is your danger, Edwy? Can I help?' She laid a hand on his knee it was a slim hand but with strong blunt like fingers—'I wantto, I really do.'

'Uh-huh.' He shook his head. 'I'm not going to tell you more than I must, because if people realize you know anything you'll become a poker chip, too.' He had to use the English phrase, only chess had survived of the games he knew, but she got the idea. 'And don't try to deduce things either. I tell you, it's dangerous.'

There was no calculation in the way she got up and leaned over him and brushed his cheek with one hand. 'I'm sorry,' she whispered. 'It must be dreadful for you.'

'I'll survive. Let's continue the roundup. I mean you well, but right now I'm under a sedative. It was a shock seeing you, and it's going to go on being a shock for a while. Keep in the background, Marin; duck for cover if I start throwing things. Don't try to be sympathetic, just let me alone. Savvy?'

She nodded mutely.

In spite of the drug, his voice roughened. There was still a knife in him. 'You can sleep in that room there.'

'All right,' she said quietly. 'I understand. If you change your mind, I'll understand that, too.' After a moment: 'You could have my appearance altered again, you know.'

He didn't reply, but sat wondering. It was the logical answer— No. He would always remember. He didn't believe in hiding from a fact.

The door chimed and said: 'Minister Chanthavar Tang vo Lurin wishes to see you, sir.' The scanner screen flashed an image of the agent's face; it was taut and cold with a choked anger.

'All right. Send him in.' Marin went into another room. Langley did not rise as Chanthavar entered, and sat waiting for the other to speak first.

'You saw Brannoch today.'

Langley raised his brows. The coolness was still on him, but it only made his stiff-necked resentment more controlled. 'Is that illegal?' he asked.

'What did he want of you?'

'What do you think? The same as Valti and you and everybody else wants. I told him no, because I haven't anything to give.'

Chanthavar's sleek dark head cocked forward. 'Haven't you?' he snapped. 'I wonder! I wonder very much. So far my superiors have kept me from opening your mind. They claim that if you don't know, if you really haven't figured it out, the procedure will keep you from ever doing so. It's not a pleasant experience. You won't be quite the same man afterward.'

'Go ahead,' challenged Langley. 'I can't stop you.'

'If I had time to argue my chiefs down, I would,' said Chanthavar bluntly. 'But everything's happening at once. A munitions plant on Venus was blown up today. I'm on the track of a ring which is trying to stir up the Commons and arm them. It's – Brannoch's work, of course. He's gambling his whole organization, just to keep me too busy to find Saris. Which suggests he has reason to believe Saris can be found.'

'I tell you, I've thought about it till I'm blue in the face, and . . . I . . . don't . . . know.' Langley met the wrathful black eyes with a hard gray stare. 'Don't you think I'm smart enough to save myself a lot of trouble? If I did know, I'd tell somebody or other, I wouldn't horse around this way.'

'That may be,' said Chanthavar grimly. 'Nevertheless, I

warn you that if you haven't offered some logical suggestion
within another couple of days, I'll take it on myself to have
you interrogated. The hunt's going on, but we can't scour
every nook and cranny of a whole world – especially with so
many powerful Ministers fussy about having their private
estates searched. But Saris will be found if I have to rip the
planet apart – and you with it.'

'I'll do my best,' said Langley. 'This is my planet too, you
know.'

'All right. I'll settle for that, but *very* temporarily. Now,
one other thing. My watchers report a female slave was sent
you by Brannoch. I want to see her.'

'Look here—'

'Shut up. Fetch her out.'

Marin entered of herself. She bowed to Chanthavar and
then stood quietly under the rake of his eyes. There was a
long stillness.

'So,' whispered the agent. 'I think I see. Langley, what are
your reactions to this? Do you want to keep her?'

'I do. If you won't agree, I'll guarantee to do my best to
see you never find Saris. But I'm not going to swap a whole
civilization just for her, if that's what you're thinking.'

'No . . . it isn't. I'm not afraid of that.' Chanthavar stood
with feet wide apart, hands clasped behind his back,
scowling at the floor. 'I wonder what his idea really is? Some
of his own brand of humor? I don't know. I'll have her
guarded, too.'

He was silent for a while. Langley wondered what was
going on inside that round skull. And then he looked up
with elfish merriment in his eyes.

'Never mind!' said Chanthavar. 'I just thought of a joke.
Sit back and do some hard thinking, captain. I've got to go
now. Good day to you both – enjoy yourselves.' He bowed
crisply and went out.

CHAPTER ELEVEN

THE rain stopped near sunset, but there were still clouds
and blackness overlay the city. Langley and Marin ate a
lonely supper in their apartment. With the sedative worn off,
the man had to focus his mind on impersonalities, he dared
not think of her as a fully human being yet. He flung questions at her, and she answered. What he learned tended to
confirm Valti's account of the Society: it really was a nomad
culture, patriarchal and polygamous, owning warships but
behaving peacefully; its rulers really were unknown, its early
history obscure. She gave a less favorable account of Centaurian culture and intentions than Brannoch's, but, of
course, that was only to be expected.

'Two interstellar imperialisms, moving on a collision
course,' said Langley. 'Thor really does seem better to me
than Earth, but— Maybe I'm prejudiced.'

'You can't help it,' said Marin seriously. 'Thorian society
has an archaic basis, it's closer to what you knew in your
period than modern Earth. Still, it's hard to imagine them
making much progress, if they should win out. They've been
frozen too, nothing really new happening, for a good five
hundred years now.'

'What price progress?' shrugged Langley. 'I've gotten
pessimistic about change for the sake of change; a petrified
civilization may be the only final answer for man, provided
it's reasonably humane. I don't see much to choose between
either of the great powers today.'

Unquestionably, the conversation was being recorded, but
he no longer gave a damn.

'It would be nice to find a little mousehole and crawl into
it and forget all this fighting,' said Marin wistfully.

'That's what ninety-nine per cent of the human race has

always wanted to do, I think,' said Langley. 'The fact that they try to bring on their own punishment for being lazy and cowardly – rulers who flog them into action. There will never be peace and freedom till every individual man out of a majority, at least, is prepared to think for himself and act accordingly; and I'm becoming afraid that day will never come.'

'They say there are thousands of lost colonies,' answered Marin softly, with a dream in her eyes. 'Thousands of little groups who went off to find their own particular kind of utopia. Surely one of them, somewhere, has become something different.'

'Perhaps. But we're here, not there.' Langley got up. 'Let's turn in. Good night, Marin.'

'Good night,' she said. Her smile was shy, as if she were still unsure how he looked at her.

Alone in his room, Langley donned pajamas, crawled into bed, and got out a cigarette. It was time for him to decide. Chanthavar had given him a couple of days; he couldn't bluff any longer, because he was reasonably sure he did have the answer about Saris. There'd be no use in undergoing the personality-wrecking degradation of a mental probe.

More and more, it seemed that the only logical action was to tell Chantavar. From the standpoint of personal safety: he was, after all, on Earth; in spite of the nets woven by Brannoch and Valti, the dominating power here was Chanthavar's. Going to someone else would involve all the risks of contact and escape.

From the standpoint of humanitarianism: Sol was defending the *status quo*; she was not openly aggressive like Centauri, but would be content to have the upper hand. If it came to war in spite of everything, the Solar System held more people than the Centaurian. It would take Brannoch almost nine years to get a message to his home and get the fleet back here; in nine years, the Saris effect could probably be turned into a standardized weapon. (And, be it noted, a relatively gentle weapon, which did not in itself harm any living creature.)

From the standpoint of history: Sol and Centauri had both reached a dead end, no choice there. The Society was too unknown, too unpredictable. Furthermore, Centauri was under the influence of Thrym, whose nature and ultimate intentions were a mystery. Sol was at least fairly straightforward.

From the standpoint of Saris Hronna, who had been Langley's friend: well, Saris was just one individual. It was better that he be vivisected, if necessary, than that a billion humans have their skin burned off and their eyes melted in a single flash of nuclear disintegration.

The safe, the obvious, the conforming course was open before Langley. Turn his deductions over to Chanthavar, find a niche for himself on Earth, and settle down to drag out his days. It would get dull after a few years, of course, but it would be safe; he'd be spared the necessity of thinking.

Well— He struck another cigarette. Sleep on it, at least, if he could sleep.

Where were Bob and Jim? In what darkness did they lie, full of fear? Or had they already gone down into the final night? He didn't think he'd see them again. If he knew who their murderers were, be sure that he'd kill himself before helping that side; but he would most likely spend his life in puzzled impotence.

Closing his eyes, he tried to call up the image of Peggy. She was gone, she had died so long ago that the very blood of her was thinned through the entire race. Quite possibly everyone he had met, Chanthavar and Brannoch and Valti and Marin and Yulien and the faceless Commoners huddled on low-level, stemmed from one unforgotten night with her. It was a strange thought. He wondered if she had married again; he hoped so, hoped that it had been a good man and that her life had been happy, but it wasn't likely.

He tried to see her before him, but it was hard to get a clear vision. Marin overlay it, they were like two pictures one on the other and not quite in line, the edges blurred. Peggy's smile had never been just like what he saw now – or had it?

He swore in a dull tone, snubbed out the cigarette, and turned off the light which glowed from walls and ceiling. Sleep would not come, he lay restlessly with a rusty chain of thought dragging through his skull.

It might have been hours later when he heard the explosion.

He sat up in bed, staring blindly before him. That had been a blaster going off! What the devil—?

Another crash sounded, and boots slammed on the floor. Langley jumped to his feet. Armed force – a real kidnap try this time, in spite of all guards! Another energy bolt flamed somewhere outside the room, and he heard a deep-voiced oath.

He crouched against the farther wall, doubling his fists. No lights. If they were after him, let them find and haul him out.

The tumult rolled somewhere in the living room. Then he heard Marin scream.

He sprang for the door. 'Open, damn you!' It sensed him and dilated. A metal-clad arm slapped him back, down to the floor.

'Stay where you are, sir.' It was a hoarse gasp out of the masklike combat helmet. 'They've broken in—'

'Let me *go!*' Langley shoved against the gigantic form of the Solar cop. He was no match, the slave stood like a rock.

'Sorry, sir, my orders—'

A blue-white beam snapped across the field of view. Langley had a glimpse of a spacesuited figure hurtling out the smashed window, and Marin writhing in its arms. Other police were charging after it, firing wildly.

Then, slowly, there was silence.

The guard bowed. 'They're gone now, sir. Come on out if you wish.'

Langley stepped into the shambles of his living room. There was a haze of smoke, burned plastic, the thin bitter reek of ozone. Furniture was trampled wreckage between the bulky, armored shapes which filled the chamber.

'What happened?' he yelled.

'Easy, sir.' The squad commander threw back his helmet; the shaven head looked tiny, poking out of the metal and fabric that incased its body. 'You're all right. Would you like a sedative?'

'I asked you what happened!' Langley wanted to smash the impassive face. 'Go on, tell me, I order you.'

'Very good, sir. Two small, armed spaceships attacked us just outside.' The commander pointed to the sharded window. 'While one engaged our boats, the other discharged several men in space armor with antigravity flying units, who broke into the suite. Some of them stood off our reinforcements coming through the door – one of them grabbed your slave – then we rallied, more men came, and they retreated. No casualties on either side, I believe; it was a very brief action. Luckily they failed to get you, sir.'

'Who were they?'

'I don't know, sir. Their equipment was not standard for any known military or police force. I think one of our aircraft has slapped a tracer beam on them, but it can't follow them outside the atmosphere and that's doubtless where they'll go. But relax, sir. You're safe.'

Yeah. Safe. Langley choked and turned away. He felt drained of strength.

Chanthavar showed up within an hour. His face was carefully immobile as he surveyed the ruin. 'They got away, all right,' he said. 'But it doesn't matter too much, since they failed.'

'Who were they, do you know?' asked Langley dully.

'No, I couldn't say. Probably Centaurian, possibly Society. It'll be investigated, of course.' Chanthavar struck a cigarette. 'In a way, it's a hopeful sign. When a spy resorts to strongarm methods, he's usually getting desperate.'

'Look here.' Langley grabbed his arm. 'You've got to find them. You've got to get that girl back. Do you understand?'

Chanthavar drew hard on his cigarette, sucking in his cheeks till the high bones stood out. His eyes were speculative on the American. 'So she means that much to you already?' he asked.

'No— Well— It's plain decency! You can't let her be torn apart by them, looking for something she doesn't know.'

'She's only a slave,' shrugged Chanthavar. 'Apparently, she was snatched impulsively when they were repelled from your quarters. It doesn't mean a thing. I'll give you a duplicate of her if it's that important to you.'

'*No!*'

'All right, have it your way. But if you try to trade information for her—'

'I won't,' said Langley. His lie had become a mechanical reflex. 'I haven't anything to trade – not yet, anyway.'

'I'll do everything in my power,' said Chanthavar. He clapped Langley's shoulder with a brief, surprising friendliness. 'Now back to bed for you. I prescribe twelve hours' worth of sleep-drug.'

Langley took it without protest. It would be something to escape the sense of his own utter helplessness. He fell into an abyss without dreams, without memory.

Waking, he found that repairs had been made while he slept; the fight last night might never have happened. Afternoon sunlight gleamed off the ships patrolling beyond his window. A doubled guard. Locking the barn door – no, the horse hadn't been stolen after all, had it?

His mind gnawed the problem like a starving dog with an

old bone from which all nourishment has gone. Marin ...
because she had come near him, she was gone into darkness;
because she had been kind to him, she was given over to fear
and captivity and torment. So this was how it felt to be a
Jonah.

Was it only that she looked like Peggy? Was it herself?
Was it the principle of the thing? Whatever the anguish in
him derived from, it was there.

He thought of calling Brannoch, calling Valti, throwing
his accusation into their faces and— And what? They would
deny it. He would surely not be allowed to go see them any
more. Several times he called Chanthavar's office, to be informed by a maddeningly polite secretary that he was out on
business. He smoked endlessly, paced the floor, threw himself into a chair and got up again. Now and then he ran
through his whole stock of curses and obscenities. None of it
helped.

Night came, and he drugged himself into another long
sleep. Drugs might be the way he ended up – or suicide,
quicker and cleaner. He thought of stepping out on his balcony and over the side. That would finish the whole mess. A
well-designed robot would mop up his spattered remnants
and for him this universe would no longer exist.

In the afternoon, a call came. He sprang for the phone,
stumbled, fell to the floor, and got up swearing. The hand
that switched it on shook uncontrollably.

Chanthavar's face smiled with an unusual warmth. 'I've
got good news for you, captain,' he said, 'we've found the
girl.'

Briefly, his mind would not accept it. The weary groove of
futility was worn so deep that he could not climb out. He
stared, open-mouthed, hearing the words as if from far
away:

'... She was sitting on a bridgeway, rather dazed, when
picked up. Post-anesthetic reaction, she's coming out of it

already. There was no deep mental probing done, I'm sure, perhaps only a mild narcosynthesis – no harm done at all that I can see. She's been unconscious all the time, doesn't know a thing. I'm sending her over now.' Chanthavar grinned.

The impact trickled slowly through the barriers of craziness. Langley knelt, wanting to cry or pray or both, but nothing would come out. Then he began to laugh.

The hysteria had faded by the time she entered. But it was the most natural thing in the world to embrace her. She held him close, shaking with reaction.

Finally they sat together on a couch, holding hands. She told him what she could. 'I was seized, carried into the ship, someone pointed a stun gun at me and then there's nothing more. The next thing I remember is sitting on the bridgeway bench, being carried along. I must have been put onto it, led there in a sleep-walking state, and left. I felt dizzy. Then a policeman came and took me to Minister Chanthavar's office. He asked me questions, had me given a medical checkup, and said nothing seemed wrong. So he sent me back here.'

'I don't get it,' said Langley. 'I don't understand it at all.'

'Minister Chanthavar said apparently I was taken on the chance I might be of value ... when they failed to get you. I was kept unconscious so I wouldn't be able to identify anybody, asked a few simple questions under narcosynthesis, and released when it was clear I could be of no help.' She sighed, smiling a little tremulously at him. 'I'm glad they let me go.' He knew she didn't mean it only for herself.

He swallowed the drink he had prepared and sat without speaking for a while. His mind felt oddly clarified, but the past hours of nightmare underlay it.

So this was what it meant. This was what Sol and Centauri stood for, a heartless power game, where no one counted, no act was too vile. A stiffened robot of a civilization which should have been long in its grave but walked with corruption under its armor; a brawling, killing barbarism, stagnant and sterile even as it boasted of virility; a few ambitious men, and a billion harmless humans turned into radioactive gas. The moment one side felt it had an advantage, it would be on the other's back, and the struggle would lay planets waste. This was what he was supposed to sanction.

He still knew little about the Society; they were surely no collection of pure-minded altruists. But it did seem that they were neutral, that they had no lunacies about empire. Surely they knew more of the galaxy, had a better chance of finding him some young world where he could again be a man.

His choice was clear. It would run him through a gamut of death, but there are worse things than extinction.

He looked at the clean profile of the girl beside him. He wanted to ask her what she thought, what she desired. He hardly knew her at all. But he couldn't, with the listening mechanical ears. He would have to decide for her.

She met his gaze with calm green eyes. 'I wish you'd tell me what's going on, Edwy,' she said. 'I seem to be as exposed as you in any case, and I'd like to know.'

He gave in and told her of Saris Hronna and the hunt for him. She grasped the idea at once, nodded without excitement, and refrained from asking him if he knew an answer or what he intended to do. 'It is a very large thing,' she said.

'Yeah,' said Langley. 'And it's going to get a lot bigger before long.'

CHAPTER TWELVE

THERE might be eyes as well as ears in the walls. Langley went to bed shortly after sunset. Spy-beams went right through the communicator, Valti had said, but he wore his pajamas anyway; blankets were no longer in use. He lay for an hour, threshing about as if unable to get to sleep. Then he commanded loud music. The recorded caterwauling should drown out a low-pitched conversation.

He hoped the stomach-knotting tension in him didn't show on his face.

Scratching, as if after an itch, he pressed the stud. Then he struck a cigarette and lay waiting.

The tiny voice was a vibration inside him, he thought about sonic beams heterodyned and focused on his skull-bones. It was distorted, but he'd know Valti's phrasing anywhere:

'Ah, Captain Langley. You do me an unprecedented honor. It is a pleasure even to be routed out of a snug bed to hear you. May I advise that you speak with your lips closed? The transmission will be clear enough.'

'All right.' There was one hopeless question which had to be asked. 'I'm prepared to bargain with you – but do you have Blaustein and Matsumoto?'

'I do not, captain. Will you take my word for that?'

'I . . . reckon so. O.K. I'll tell you where I think Saris is – mind you, it's only an informed guess – and I'll help you find him if possible. In return, I want your best efforts to rescue my friends, together with the money, protection, and transportation you offered, both for myself and one other person, a slave girl who's in this apartment with me.'

It was hard to make out whether the exultation which must be leaping through that gross form had entered the

voice: 'Very good, captain. I assure you you will not regret
this. Now as to practical considerations, you must be removed without trace.'

'I'm not sure just how that little thing's going to be done,
Valti. I think I'm more or less under house arrest.'

'Nevertheless, you shall get out tonight. Let me think— In
two hours, you and the girl will stroll out onto the balcony.
For Father's sake, make it look natural! Remain there, in
plain sight from above, no matter what happens.'

'O.K. Two hours – 2347 by my clock, right? See you!'

Now it was to wait. Langley got out another cigarette and
lay as if listening to the music. *Two hours! I'll be one gray-
haired wreck before then.*

So much could go wrong. The variable-frequency radiation of the communicator was supposedly undetectable,
but maybe not. The rescue attempt might go sour. Chanthavar might suddenly get fed up and haul him off for in-
quisition. Valti might be betrayed by spies within his own
ranks. Might, might, might! Animals are luckier than man,
they don't worry.

Time crawled, it took forever to get by a minute. Langley
swore, went into the living room, and dialed for a book.
Basic modern physics – at the rate time was going, two
hours would be enough to get a Ph.D. He grew suddenly
aware that he had been staring at the same scanned page for
fifteen minutes. Hastily he dialed the next. Even if it wasn't
registering he ought to look as if it were.

The text mentioned a name, Ynsen, credited with first
giving Riemannian space – they called it 'Sarlennian' now –
a physical meaning. After a minute, he guessed the original
form. Einstein! So something had survived of his own age,
however corrupted. He smiled, feeling a sadness within himself, and wondered what a historical novel laid in the
Twenty-first Century would read like. Probably concern the
struggle between Lincoln and Stalin for control of the Lunar
rocket bases – the hero would scoot around on his trusty

bicycle— No, there wasn't any such novel. His age was all
but forgotten, its details long eaten away by time. A few
archeologists might be interested, no one else. Imagine a
first-dynasty Egyptian brought to New Washington, 2047
A.D. He'd be a nine days' wonder, but how many people
would *care*?

He looked at the clock, and felt his belly muscles tighten.
Twenty minutes to go.

He had to get Marin outside, he couldn't leave her in this
hellhole, and he had to do it in a way that the observers
would consider unremarkable. For a while he sat thinking.
The only way was one he didn't like, a far New England
ancestor compressed angry lips and tried to stop him.
But—

He walked over to the door of her room. It opened for
him, and he stood looking down on her. She was asleep. The
coppery hair spilled softly around a face which held peace.
He tried not to remember Peggy, and touched her arm.

She sat up. 'Oh . . . Edwy.' Blinking her eyes open: 'What
is it?'

'Sorry to wake you,' he said awkwardly. 'I couldn't sleep.
Come talk to me, will you?'

She regarded him with something like compassion. 'Yes,'
she said at last. 'Yes, of course.' Throwing a cloak over her
thin nightgown, she followed him onto the balcony.

There were stars overhead. Against the remote blaze of
city lights swam the black shark-form of a patrol ship. A
small wind ruffled his hair. He wondered just where Lora
stood – not far from the ancient site of Winnipeg, wasn't
it?

Marin leaned against his side, and he put an arm about
her waist. The vague light showed a wistful, uncertain curve
to her mouth.

'It's nice out,' he said banally.

'Yes—' She was waiting for something. He knew what it

was, and so did Chanthavar's observers sitting at their screens.

He stooped and made himself kiss her. She responded gently, a little clumsily as yet. Then he looked at her for a long while, and couldn't say anything.

'I'm sorry,' he mumbled at last.

How long to go – five minutes? Ten?

'What for?' she asked.

'I've no right—'

'You have every right. I'm yours, you know. This is what I'm for.'

'Shut up!' he croaked. 'I mean a moral right. Slavery is wrong no matter how you set it up. I've ancestors who died at Gettysburg, in Germany, in the Ukraine, because there was slavery.'

'You mean you don't want to force yourself on me,' she said. 'It's good of you, but don't worry. I've been conditioned – I like the idea, it's my function.'

'Exactly. It's still enslavement – a worse one, I think, than just putting chains on you. No!'

She laid her hands on his shoulders, and the gaze that met his was calm and serious. 'Forget that,' she said. 'Everybody's conditioned – you, I, everybody, life does that one way or another. It doesn't count. But you need me, and I . . . I'm very fond of you, Edwy. Every woman wants a man. Isn't that enough?'

There was a hammering in his temples.

'Come,' she said, taking his hand, 'come on back inside.'

'No . . . not yet,' he stammered.

She waited. And because there seemed nothing else to do, he found himself kissing her again.

Five minutes? Three? Two? One?

'Come,' she breathed, 'come with me now.'

He hung back. 'Wait . . . wait—'

'You aren't afraid of me. What is it? There's something strange—'

'Shut up!' he gasped.

Fire blossomed in the air. A moment later Langley felt a fist of concussion. He lurched back, and saw a spaceship streak by, blazing at the patrol craft. Wind roared behind it.

'*Get out of the way, Edwy—*' Marin darted for the shelter of the living room. He grabbed her by the hair, snatched her back, and stood in the open. The attacking ship fled, gone in a blur.

And something took hold of Langley and whirled him upward.

Tractor beam, he thought crazily, *a controlled gravity beam—* Then something black yawned before him, a portal gaped, he went through and it clanged shut behind him.

There was a pulsing of great engines as he picked himself up. Marin huddled at his feet, he raised her and she shuddered in his arms. 'It's all right,' he mumbled shakily. 'It's all right. We got away. Maybe.'

A man in gray coveralls entered the little steel lock chamber. 'Well done, sir!' he said. 'I think we're pulling clear. Will you follow me?'

'What is it?' asked Marin wildly. 'Where are we going?'

'I made a deal with the Society,' said Langley. 'They'll get us out of the Solar System – we're going to be free, both of us.'

Inwardly, he wondered.

They went down a narrow hall. The ship thrummed around them. It must be accelerating furiously, but there was no sense of pressure: a countering gravity field generated within the hull, or perhaps the drive acting equally on all masses aboard. At the end of the passage, they came into a small room studded and glittering with instruments. One screen held a complete view of the hard stars of space.

Goltam Valti surged from his chair to pound Langley's back and pump his hand and roar a greeting. 'Marvelous, captain! Excellent! A lovely job, if you pardon my immodesty.'

Langley felt weak. He sat down, pulling Marin to his lap without thinking about it. 'Just exactly what did happen?' he asked.

'I and a few others slipped out of the Society tower,' said Valti. 'We took an air speedster to the estate of a ... sympathetic ... Minister, where we maintain a little bastion. Two spaceships were required: one to create a brief diversion, and this one to pull you up and escape in the confusion.'

'How about the other boat? Won't they catch that?'

'It has been arranged for. There will be a lucky shot which brings it down – bomb planted aboard, you know. It's robot manned, carefully cleaned of all traces of ownership except one or two small indications which may suggest Centaurian origin to Chanthavar.' Valti winced. 'A pity to lose so fine a vessel. It cost a good half-million solars. Profits are hard to come by these days, believe me, sir.'

'As soon as Chanthavar checks on you, finds you missing—'

'My good captain!' Valti looked hurt. 'I am not *quite* an amateur. You see, my double is already peacefully and lawfully asleep in my own quarters.

'Of course,' he added thoughtfully, 'if we can find Saris, it may well be necessary for me to leave Sol altogether. If so, I do hope my successor can handle the Venusian trade. It's a difficult one, it can so easily go into the red.'

'All right,' said Langley. 'It's done. I'm committed. What's your plan of action?'

'That depends on where he is and what methods will be required to establish contact. But this flitter is fast, silent, screened against radiation; it has weapons, and there are thirty armed men aboard. Do you think it will suffice?'

'I ... believe so. Bring me some maps of the Mesko area.'

Valti nodded at the little green-furred creature Thakt, which had been sitting in a corner. It tittered and scuttled out.

'Charming young lady,' bowed Valti. 'May I ask her name?'

'Marin,' she said in a thin voice. She got off Langley's lap and stood backed against the wall.

'It's all right,' said the spaceman. 'Don't be afraid.'

'I'm not afraid, ' she said, trying to smile. 'But bewildered.'

Thakt returned with a sheaf of papers. Langley frowned over them, attempting to find his way through an altered geography. 'It was one time on Holat,' he said. 'Saris and I had taken the day off to go fishing, and he showed me some caves. I told him about Carlsbad Caverns in New Mexico, and he was very interested. Later, shortly before we left for Earth, he mentioned them again, and I promised to take him there; and as we were going over some maps of Earth, for the benefit of several Holatan philosophers, I showed him their location. So if he could get maps of the modern world – Carlsbad wouldn't be far away, and he'd know it was an unexplored warren. Of course, it may be colonized or something by now, or have gone out of existence, for all I know, but—'

Valti followed his pointing finger. 'Yes ... I believe I've heard of the spot,' he said with a touch of excitement. 'Corrad Caverns ... yes, here. Is that the location?'

Langley used a large-scale map to orient himself. 'I think so.'

'Ah, then I do know. It's part of the estate of Minister Ranull, who keeps a good deal of his property in a wild desert condition as a park. Sometimes his guests are shown Corrad Caverns, but I'm sure that nobody ever goes very far into them, and they must be quite deserted the rest of the time. A brilliant suggestion, captain! My compliments.'

'If it doesn't pan out,' said Langley, 'then I'm just as much in the dark as you.'

'We'll try. You shall have your reward regardless.' Valti spoke into a communicator. 'We'll go there at once. No time to lose. Would you like a stimulant drug? ... Here. It will give you alertness and energy for the next several hours, and you may need them. Excuse me, I have some details to arrange.' He left, and Langley was alone with Marin. She watched him for a while without speaking.

'All right,' he said. 'All right, I made my choice. I figured the Society would make better use of this power than anybody else. But of course, you're a citizen of Sol. If you don't approve, I'm sorry.'

'I don't know. It is a very great burden to take on yourself.' She shook her head. 'I can see what led you to it — maybe you are right, maybe not, I can't say. But I'm with you, Edwy.'

'Thank you,' he said, shakenly, and wondered if, in spite of himself, he might not be falling in love with her. He had a sudden image of the two of them, starting again somewhere beyond the sky.

If they got away from Sol, of course!

CHAPTER THIRTEEN

IT had felt good to shed his over-colorful pajamas for a spaceman's coverall, boots, helmet, a gun — Langley had never quite realized how much clothes make the man. But walking through a hollow immensity of darkness, feeling the underground chill and hearing a mockery of echoes, he knew again the helplessness and self-doubt which had been strangling him.

There were light-tubes strung throughout miles of the caverns, but a sneak expedition could not turn them on; they served only to indicate regions where Saris would surely not be. Half a dozen men walked beside Langley, the reflected glow of flashbeams limning their faces ghostly against shadow. They were all crewmen, strangers to him; Valti had declared himself too old and cowardly to enter the tunnels, Marin had wanted to come but been refused permission.

A tumbled fantasy of limestone, great rough pillars and snags, leaped from the gloom as beams flashed around. This place couldn't have changed much, thought Langley. In five thousand years, the slow drip and evaporation of cold water would have added a bit here and there, but Earth was old and patient. He felt that time itself lay buried somewhere in these reaching leagues.

The man who carried the neural tracker looked up. 'Not a flicker yet,' he said. Unconsciously, his voice was hushed, as if the stillness lay heavy on it. 'How far down have we come? A long ways – and there are so many branches – Even if he is here, we may never find him.'

Langley went on. There was nothing else he could do. He didn't think Saris would have gone farther underground than necessary; the Holatans weren't exactly claustrophobic, but they were creatures of open land and sky, it went against their instincts to remain long enclosed. The alien would be after an easily defensible site with at least a couple of emergency boltholes: say a small cave having two or three tunnels out from it to the surface. But that could be any of a hundred places down here, and no map of the system was available.

Logic helped somewhat. Saris hadn't had a map of the caves either. He'd have slipped in through the main entrance, like his present followers, because he wouldn't have known where any other approach was. Then he would look for a room to live in, with exits and a water supply. Langley turned to the man with the dowsing unit. 'Isn't there a pool or river somewhere near?'

'Yes – water over in that direction. Shall we try?'

'Uh-huh.' Langley groped toward the nearest tunnel. Beyond, the passage narrowed rapidly until he had to crawl.

'This may be it,' he said. Echoes shivered around his words. 'Saris could easily slip through, he can go four-footed anytime he wants, but it's a hard approach for a man.'

'Wait . . . here, you take the tracker, captain,' said someone behind him. 'I think it kicked over, but all these people ahead of me make too much interference.'

Langley squirmed around to grasp the box. Focusing it, he squinted at the green-glowing dial. It was responsive to the short-range impulses emitted by a nervous system and – yes, the needle was quivering more than it should!

Excited, he crawled farther, the harsh damp wall scraping his back. His flashbeam was a single white lance thrust into blindness. His breathing was a loud rasp in his throat.

He came suddenly to the end and almost went over. The tunnel must open several feet or yards above the floor. 'Saris!' he called. The echoes flew about, this was a good-sized room. Somewhere he heard running water. 'Saris Hronna! Are you there?'

A blaster bolt smashed after him. He saw the dazzle of it, there were spots dancing before his eyes for minutes afterward, and the radiation stung his face. He snapped off the light and jumped, hoping wildly that it wasn't too far to the ground. Something raked his leg, the jolting impact rattled his teeth, and he fell to an invisible floor.

Another beam flamed toward the tunnel mouth. Langley felt blood hot and sticky on his calf. The Holatan knew just where the opening was, he could ricochet his bolts and fry the men within. 'Saris! It's me – Edward Langley – I'm your friend!'

The echoes laughed at him, dancing through an enormous night. *Friend, friend, friend, friend*. The underground stream talked with a cold frantic voice. If the outlaw had gone mad with fear and loneliness, or if he had decided in bleak sanity to kill any human who ventured here, Langley was done. The incandescent sword of an energy beam, or the sudden closing of jaws in his throat, would be the last thing he ever felt. It had to be tried. Langley dug himself flat against the rock. 'Saris! I've come to get you out of here! I've come to take you home!'

The answer rumbled out of blackness, impossible to locate through the echoes: 'Iss you? What do you want?'

'I've made arrangements . . . you can get back to Holat—' Langley was shouting in English, their only common language; the Holatan dialects were too unlike man's for him to have learned more than a few phrases. 'We're your friends, the only friends you've got.'

'Sso.' He could not read any expression into the tone. He thought he could feel the vibrations of a heavy body, flitting through the dark on padded feet. 'I can not be sure. Pleasse to the present situation wit' honesty describe.'

Langley put it into a few words. The stone under his belly was wet and chill. He sneezed, snuffled, and reflected on the old definition of adventure as somebody else having a tough time a thousand miles away. 'It's the only chance for all of us,' he finished. 'If you don't agree, you'll stay here till you die or are dragged out.'

There was a silence, then: 'You I trust, I know you. But iss it not that thesse otherss you hawe deceiwed possible?'

'I . . . what? Oh. You mean maybe the Society is playing me for a sucker, too? Yes. It could be. But I don't think so.'

'I hawe no dessire for dissection,' said the one who waited.

'You won't be. They want to study you, see how you do what you do. You told me your thinkers back home have a pretty good idea of how it works.'

'Yes. Not'ing could from the gross anatomy of my brain
be learned. I t'ink such a machine ass your . . . friendss . . .
wish could eassily be built.' Saris hesitated, then: 'Wery well,
I musst take chancess, no matter what happenss. Let it be
sso. You may all enter.'

When the lights picked him out, he stood tall and proud,
waiting with the dignity of his race among the boxes of supplies which had been his only reliance. He took Langley's
hands between his and nuzzled the man's cheek. 'Iss good to
see you again,' he said.

'I'm . . . sorry for what happened,' said Langley. 'I didn't
know—'

'No. The uniwerse full of surprisses iss. No matter, if I can
go home again.'

The spacemen accepted him almost casually, they were
used to non-human intelligence. After binding Langley's
injury, they formed a cordon and returned. Valti raised ship
as soon as all were aboard, and then conferred with them. 'Is
there anything you require, Saris Hronna?' he asked
through the American.

'Yess. Two witaminss which seem to be lacking in Eart'
chemistry.' Saris drew diagrams on a sheet of paper. 'Thesse
iss the structural formulass in Langley'ss symbology.'

The spaceman re-drew them in modern terms, and Valti
nodded. 'They should be easy to synthesize. I have a mol-
ecule maker in my hideaway.' He tugged at his beard. 'We
must go there first, to make preparations for departure. I
have a light-speed cruiser in a secret orbit. You'll be put
aboard that and sent to our base in the 61 Cygni system.
That's well outside the Solar and Centaurian spheres of
influence. Then your abilities can be studied at leisure, sir,
and your own payment rendered, Captain Langley.'

Saris spoke up. He had his own bargain to make. He
would coöperate if he was afterward returned to Holat with
a crew of technicians and ample supplies. His world lay too

far off to be in direct danger from the stars of this region, but some party of wandering conquistadors might happen on it – and Holat had no defenses against bombardment from space. That situation must be rectified. Armed robot satellites would not stop a full-dress invasion fleet – nothing would do that except possibly another fleet – but would be able to dispose of the small marauding groups which were all that Holat really had to worry about.

Valti winced. 'Captain, does he realize what the bonuses for a trip of that length are? Does he know how much it would cost to set up those stations? Has he no sympathy for a poor old man who must face an audit of his books?'

' 'Fraid not,' said Langley with a grin.

'Ah ... what assurances does he want that we will keep our end of such an agreement?'

'He'll have control over your development of the nullifier – you can't make it without him, both his empirical evidence and his theoretical knowledge – so that part's taken care of. When he sees the project nearing the end, he'll want your ships prepared for him, ready to go. And he'll want a bomb planted on the one carrying him, under his control; women and children will stay aboard while the work is being done for Holat, and at the first sign of treachery he'll blow the whole thing up.'

'Dear me!' Valti shook a doleful head. 'What a nasty suspicious mind he has, to be sure. I should think one look at my honest face— Well, well, so be it. But I shudder to think what the expense is going to do to our cost accounting.'

'Man, you can amortize that debt over two thousand years. Forget it. Now, where are we going first?'

'We maintain a small hideaway in the Himalayas: nothing palatial, our tastes are humble, but securely hidden. I must render a report to my chiefs on Earth, get their approval of the plan, and prepare documents for the Cygni office. It will only take a little while.'

Langley went off to the ship's sick bay. He'd taken a nasty gash in his leg, but treatment was routine these days: a clamp to hold the edges of the wound together, a shot of artificial enzymes to stimulate regeneration. In a few hours, the most radical surgery could be completely and scarlessly healed.

He remarked on that to Valti as they sat over dinner. The ship was taking a wide ellipse through space before returning to Earth, to avoid possible detection. 'I'm a little at sea about the notion of progress,' he confessed. 'Offhand, it looks as if man hasn't improved a bit; and then I see advances like you have in medicine, and think what a tremendous change for the better was made by innovations like agriculture and the machine. Maybe it's just that I'm too impatient; maybe, given a few more millennia, man will do something about himself, change his own mind from animal to human.'

Valti took a noisy slurp of beer. 'I cannot share your optimism, my friend,' he answered. 'I was born more than six hundred years ago, by skipping across space and time I have seen much history, and it seems to me that civilization – any civilization, on any planet – is subject to a law of mortality. No matter how clever we get, we will never create mass-energy, grow nothing, never make heat flow of itself from a colder to a warmer body. There are limitations set by natural law. As ships and buildings are made bigger, more of their volume must go into passageways, until you reach a limit. You could not have an immortal man; even if biochemistry permitted, he has only so much brain space, so many cells which can record his experiences. Why, then, an immortal civilization, or a civilization embracing the entire universe?'

'And so there'll always be rise, and decay, and fall – always war and suffering?'

'Either that, or the sort of thing the Technon wants: death disguised by a mechanical semblance of life. I think you look at it from the wrong angle. Is not this very change, this anguished toppling into doom, the stuff of life? There is a unity in the cosmos which is more important than any one world, any one race. I think life arose because the universe needs it, needs just those characteristics which hurt the living individual. No ... I don't believe in Father. There is no consciousness except in organic life. And yet an inanimate universe brought forth life and all its variety, because that was a necessary step in the evolution from a great cloud of gas to the final clinkered vacuum.' Valti wiped his nose and chuckled. 'Pardon me. I maunder in my old age. But if you had traveled across light-years all your days, you'd know that there is something operating which can't be reduced to physical theory. I think the Society will last because of being divorced from space and time; but only it, and even its span is not eternal.'

He got up. 'Excuse me. We'll be landing soon.'

Langley found Marin in the amidships saloon. He sat down beside her and took her hand. 'It won't be long now,' he said. 'I think we've done what's best – removed Saris' power from the place where it could only cause destruction. Best thing for Sol, too. And now we're bound on our own way.'

'Yes.' She didn't look at him. Her face was white, and there was a strained expression on it.

'What's the matter?' he asked anxiously. 'Aren't you feeling well?'

'I ... I don't know, Edwy. Everything seems so odd, somehow, as if this were a dream.' She stared cloudily before her. 'Is it? Am I sleeping somewhere and—'

'No. What is the trouble? Can't you describe it?'

She shook her head. 'It's as if someone else were sharing my brain, sitting there and waiting. It came on me all of a sudden. The strain, I suppose. I'll be all right.'

Langley scowled. Worry gnawed at him. If she took sick—

Just why was she so important to him? Was he falling for

her? It would be very easy to do. Quite apart from her looks, she was brave and intelligent and witty; he could see himself spending a contented lifetime with her.

Peggy, Jim, Bob – *No, not her, too. Not again!*

There was a small jarring shock, and the engine drone died. Saris Hronna stuck his whiskered snout through the door. 'We iss landed,' he announced. 'Come out.'

The ship lay cradled in a brightly-lit cave; behind her was a huge concrete door which must lead to the mountain slope. It would be a high, wild land, there were probably snowfields and glaciers left here on the roof of the world – cold, windy, empty, a place where men could hide for years.

'Have you any defenses?' asked Langley as Valti led the way past the hull.

'No. Why should we? They would only add more metal to be detected from above. As it is, every possible thing here is made of plastic or stone. I am a peaceful man, captain. I rely more on my cerebral cortex than my guns. In five decades, this lair has been unsuspected.'

They entered a hall off which several doors opened. Langley saw what must be a radio room, presumably for emergency use only. Valti's men wandered off toward their own quarters; they spoke little, the Society people seemed to frown on idle chatter between themselves, but they seemed quite relaxed. Why not? They were safe now. The fight was over.

Marin jerked, and her eyes widened. 'What's the matter?' asked Langley. His voice sounded hoarse and cracked.

'I . . . I don't know.' She was trying not to cry. 'I feel so strange.' Her eyes were unfocused, he saw, and she moved like a sleepwalker.

'Valti! What's wrong with her?'

'I'm afraid I don't know, captain. Probably just reaction; it's been a trying time for a person not used to conflict and suspense. Let's put her to bed and I'll get the ship's doctor to take a look at her.'

That officer admitted to puzzlement. 'Psychology is out of my field,' he explained. 'Society personnel rarely have trouble with their minds, so we have no good psychiatrists among us. I gave her a sedative. If she isn't better tomorrow, we can get a specialist.' He smiled sourly. 'Too much knowledge. Too damn much knowledge. One head can't hold it all. I can set a broken bone or cure a germ-caused disease, but when the mind goes out of kilter all I can do is mutter a few half-forgotten technical terms.'

Langley's victory crumbled in his hands.

'Come, captain,' said Valti, taking his arm, 'let's go make up Saris Hronna's vitamin pills, and after that you could probably use some sleep yourself. In twenty-four hours you'll be out of the Solar System. Think of that.'

They were working in the laboratory when Saris stiffened. 'She goess by,' he said. 'She iss walking been around and her mind feelss wery strange.'

Langley ran out into the corridor. Marin stood looking at him with clearing eyes. 'Where am I?' she said weakly.

'Come on,' he answered. 'Back to bed with you.'

'I feel better,' she told him. 'There was a pressing in my brain, everything went dark, and now I am standing here – but I feel like myself again.'

The drugged glass stood untouched by her bunk. 'Get that down,' said Langley. She obeyed, smiled at him, and went to sleep. He resisted a desire to kiss her.

Returning, he found Saris putting a flask of pills into a pouch hung about his neck. Valti had gone to do his paperwork, they were alone among the machines.

'I feeled her mind clearing ewen ass I . . . listened,' said Saris. 'Hass your race often such failingss?'

'Now and then,' said Langley. 'Gears slip. I'm afraid we aren't as carefully designed as your people.'

'You could be so. We kill the weaklingss young.'

'It's been done by my race, now and then, but the custom never lasted long. Something in our nature seems to forbid it.'

'And yet you can desstroy a world for your own ambitions. I shall newer understsand you.'

'I doubt we'll ever understand ourselves.' Langley rubbed his neck, thinking. 'Could it be that because we're non-telepaths, each of us isolated from all the others, every individual develops in his own way? Your people have their emotional empathy; the Thrymans, I've read, share thoughts directly. In cases like that, the individual is, in a way, under the control of the whole race. But in man, each of us is always alone, we have to find our own separate ways and we grow apart.'

'It may be. I am astonished at what I hawe learned of your diwersity. I sometimess t'ink your folk iss the despair and the hope of the uniwerse.'

Langley yawned. He ached with weariness, now that the stimulant had worn off. 'To hell with it. I'm for some sack time.'

He was wakened hours later by the crash of an explosion. As he sat up, he heard blasters going off.

CHAPTER FOURTEEN

ANOTHER blowup shivered through walls and into Langley's bones. Somebody screamed, somebody else cursed, and there were running feet in the corridors. As he tumbled into his clothes and snatched his energy gun out, he wanted to vomit. Somehow they had failed, somehow the rebellion of pawns was broken and the game went on.

He flattened himself against the archaic manual door of

the room given him and opened it a crack. There was a stink of burned flesh outside. Two gray-clad corpses sprawled in the passage, but the fight had swept past. Langley stepped out.

There was noise up ahead of him, toward the assembly chamber. He ran in that direction with some blind idea of opening up on the attackers from behind. A bitter wind was clearing smoke away and he gasped for breath. A remote part of him realized that the entry port had been blown open and the thin mountain air was rushing in.

Now – the doorway! He burst through, squeezing the trigger of his blaster. There was no recoil, but the beam hissed wide of the back he wanted. He didn't know how to aim a modern gun, how to outwit a modern mind, how to do anything. Understanding of the technique came just as someone spun around on a heel and kicked expertly with the other foot. Langley's blaster was torn loose, clattered to the floor, and he stared into a dozen waiting muzzles.

Valti's crew was gathered around Saris Hronna. Their hands were lifted sullenly, they had been overpowered in the assault and were giving up. The Holatan crouched on all fours, his eyes a yellow blaze.

Brannoch dhu Crombar let out a shout of Homeric laughter. 'So there you are!' he cried. 'Greetings, Captain Langley!' He towered over the tight-packed fifty of his men. The scarred face was alight with boisterous good humor. 'Come join the fun.'

'Saris—' groaned the American.

'Please.' Brannoch elbowed a way over to him. 'Credit me with some brains. I had purely mechanical weapons made for half my party, several days ago – percussion caps of mercury fulminate setting off a chemical explosion – thunderish hard to shoot straight with 'em, but at close quarters we can fill you with lead and he's powerless to stop it.'

'I see.' Langley felt surrender in himself, the buckling of all hope. 'But how did you find us?'

Marin entered. She stood in the doorway looking at them with her face congealed to a mask, the face of a slave.

Brannoch jerked a thumb at her. 'The girl, of course,' he said. 'She told us.'

Her inhuman composure ripped. 'No!' she stammered. 'I never—'

'Not consciously, my dear,' said Brannoch. 'But while you were under your final surgery, a posthypnotic command was planted by a conditioning machine. Very powerful, such an order – impossible to break it. If Saris was found, you were to notify me of the circumstances at the first opportunity. Which, I see, you did.'

She watched him with a mute horror. Langley heard a thundering in his head.

Very distantly, he made out the Centaurian's rumble: 'You might as well know, captain. It was I who took your friends. They couldn't tell me anything, and against my wishes they . . . died. I'm sorry.'

Langley turned away from him. Marin began to weep.

Valti cleared his throat. 'A nice maneuver, my lord. Very well executed. But there is the matter of several casualties among my own people. I'm afraid the Society can't permit that sort of thing. There will have to be restitution.'

'Including Saris Hronna, no doubt?' Brannoch grinned without humor.

'Of course. And reparations according to the weregild schedule set by treaty. Otherwise the Society will have to apply sanctions to your system.'

'Withdrawal of trade?' snorted Brannoch. 'We can do without your cargoes. And just try to use military force!'

'Oh, no, my lord,' said Valti mildly. 'We are a humane people. But we do have a large share in the economic life of every planet where we have offices. Investments, local companies owned by us – if necessary, we could do deplorable things to your economy. It isn't as rigid as Sol's, you know. I doubt if your people would take kindly to . . .

say . . . catastrophic inflation when we released several tons of the praseodymium which is your standard, followed by depression and unemployment when a number of key corporations retired from business.'

'I see,' said Brannoch, unmoved. 'I didn't intend to use more force on you than necessary, but you drive me to it. If your entire personnel here disappeared without trace – I'll have to think about it. I'd miss our gambling games.'

'I've already filed a report to my chiefs, my lord; I was only waiting for their final orders. They know where I am.'

'But do they know who raided you? It could be fixed to throw the blame on Chanthavar. Yes. An excellent idea.'

Brannoch turned back to Langley. He had to grip the spaceman's shoulder hard to attract his attention. 'Look here,' he asked, 'does this beast of yours speak any modern language?'

'No,' said Langley, 'and if you think I'm going to be your interpreter, you've got another think coming.'

The heavy face looked pained. 'I wish you'd stop considering me a fiend, captain. I have my duty. I don't hold any grudge against you for trying to get away from me; if you coöperate, my offer still stands. If not, I'll have to execute you, and nothing will be gained. We'll teach Saris the language and make him work anyhow. All you could do is slow us up a little.' He paused. 'I'd better warn you, though. If you try to sabotage the project once it's under way, the punishment will be stiff.'

'Go ahead, then,' said Langley. He didn't care, not any more. 'What do you want to say to him?'

'We want to take him to Thor, where he'll aid us in building a nullifier. If anything goes wrong through his doing, he'll die, and robot ships will be sent to bombard his planet. They'll take a thousand years to get there, but they'll be sent. If, on the other hand he helps us, he'll be returned home.' Brannoch shrugged. 'Why should he care which party wins out? It's not his species.'

Langley translated into English, almost word for word. Saris stood quiet for a minute, then:

'Iss grief in you, my friend.'

'Yeah,' said Langley. 'Reckon so. What do you want to do?'

The Holatan looked thoughtful. 'Iss hard to say. I hawe little choice at pressent. Yet from what I know of today'ss uniwerse, iss not best to aid Sol or Centauri.'

'Brannoch has a point,' said Langley. 'We're just another race. Except for the Society offering you a little better deal, it doesn't affect your people.'

'But it doess. Wrongness in life, anywhere in all space, iss wrongness. Iss, for instance, chance that some day someone findss out a for traweling faster than light met'od. Then one race on the wrong pat' iss a general menace. Also to itself, since other outraged planetss might unite to exterminate it.'

'Well . . . is there anything we can do, now, except get ourselves killed in a fit of messy heroism?'

'No. I see no out-way. That doess not mean none exists. Best to follow the scent ass laid, while snuffing after a new track.'

Langley nodded indifferently. He was too sick of the whole slimy business to care much as yet. Let the Centaurians win. They were no worse than anybody else. 'O.K., Brannoch,' he said. 'We'll string along.'

'Excellent!' The giant shivered, as if with a nearly uncontrollable exuberance.

'You realize, of course,' said Valti, 'that this means war.'

'What else?' asked Brannoch, honestly surprised.

'A war which, with or without nullifiers, could wreck civilization in both systems. How would you like, say, the Procyonites to come take over the radioactive ruins of Thor?'

'All life is a gamble,' said Brannoch. 'If you didn't load your dice and mark your cards – I know blazing well you do, too! – you'd see that. So far the balance of power has been pretty even. Now we will have the nullifier; it may tip the scales very far indeed, if we use it right. It's not a final weapon, but it's potent.' He threw back his head and shook with silent laughter.

Recovering himself: 'All right. I've got a little den of my own, in Africa. We'll go there first to make preliminary arrangements – among other things, a nice convincing synthetic dummy, Saris' corpse, for Chanthavar to find. I can't leave Earth right away, or he'd suspect too much. The thing to do is tip my hand just enough to get declared *persona non grata*, leave in disgrace – and come back with a fleet behind me!'

Langley found himself hustled outside, onto a slope where snow crackled underfoot and the sky was a dark vault of stars. His breath smoked white from his mouth, breathing was keen and cold, his body shuddered. Marin crept near him, as if for warmth, and he stepped aside from her. *Tool!*

No . . . no, he wasn't being fair to her, was he? She had been under a gas when she betrayed him, with less will of her own than if someone had held a gun at her back. But he couldn't look at her now without feeling unclean.

A spaceship hovered just off the ground. Langley walked up the ladder, found himself a chair in the saloon, and tried not to think. Marin gave him a glance full of pain and then took a seat away from the others. A couple of armed guards, arrogant blond men who must be Thorians themselves, lounged at the doors. Saris had been taken elsewhere. He was not yet helpless, but his only possible action would be the suicidal one of crashing the ship, and Brannoch seemed willing to chance that.

The mountains fell away under their keel. There was a brief booming of sundered air, and then they were over the atmosphere, curving around the planet toward central Africa.

Langley wondered what he was going to do with himself, all the remaining days of his life. Quite possibly Brannoch would establish him on some Earth-type world as promised – but it would be inside the range of his own and Solar culture, marked for eventual conquest, it would not be what he had imagined. Well—

He wouldn't see the war, but all his life there would be nightmares in which the sky tore open and a billion human creatures were burned, flayed, gutted, and baked into the ground. And yet what else could he have done? He had tried, and failed . . . wasn't it enough?

No, said the New England ancestor.

But I didn't ask for the burden.

No man asks to be born, and nevertheless he must bear his own life.

I tried, I tell you!

Did you try hard enough? You will always wonder.

What can I do?

You can refuse to surrender.

Time slipped by; so many minutes closer to his death, he thought wearily. Africa was on the dayside now, but Brannoch's ship went down regardless: Langley supposed that something had been flanged up, fake recognition signals maybe, to get it by the sky patrols. There was a viewscreen, and he watched a broad river which must be the Congo. Neat plantations stretched in orderly squares as far as he could see, and scattered over the continent were medium-sized cities. The ship ignored them, flying low until it reached a small cluster of dome-shaped buildings.

'Ah,' said Valti. 'A plantation administrative center – perfectly genuine too, I have no doubt. But down underground, hm-m-m.'

A section of dusty earth opened metal lips and the ship descended into a hangar. Langley followed the rest out and into the austere rooms beyond. At the end of the walk there was a very large chamber; it held some office equipment and a tank.

Langley studied the tank with a glimmer of interest. It was a big thing, a steel box twenty feet square by fifty long, mounted on its own antigravity sled. There were auxiliary bottles for gas, pumps, engines, meters, a dial reading an internal pressure which he translated as over a thousand atmospheres. Nice trick, that . . . was it done by force-fields, or simply today's metallurgy? The whole device was a great, self-moving machine, crouched there as if it were a living thing.

Brannoch stepped ahead of the party and waved gaily at it. His triumph had given him an almost boyish swagger. 'Here they are, you Thrymkas,' he said. 'We bagged every one of them!'

CHAPTER FIFTEEN

THE flat microphonic voice answered bleakly: 'Yes. Now, are you certain that no traps have been laid, that you have not been traced, that everything is in order?'

'Of course!' Brannoch's glee seemed to nose-dive; all at once, he looked sullen. 'Unless you were seen flying your tank here.'

'We were not. But after arrival, we made an inspection. The laxity of the plantation superintendent which means yours – has been deplorable. In the past week he has bought two new farm hands and neglected to condition them against remembering whatever they see of us and our activities.'

'Oh, well – plantation slaves! They'll never see the compound anyway.'

'The probability is small, but it exists and it can be guarded against. The error has been rectified, but you will order the superintendent put under five minutes of neural shock.'

'Look here—' Brannoch's lips drew back from his teeth. 'Mujara has been in my pay for five years, and served faithfully. A reprimand is enough, I won't have—'

'You will.'

For a moment longer the big man stood defiantly, as if before an enemy. Then something seemed to bend inside him, and he shrugged and smiled with a certain bitterness. 'Very well. Just as you say. No use making an issue of it; there's enough else to do.'

Langley's mind seemed to pick itself up and start moving again. He still felt hollow, drained of emotion, but he could think and his reflections were not pleasant. *Valti was hinting at this. Those gazabos in that glorified ashcan aren't just Brannoch's little helpers. They're the boss. In their own quiet way, they're running this show.*

But what do they want out of it? Why are they bothering? How can they gain by brewing up a war? The Thorians could use more land, but an Earth-type planet's no good to a hydrogen breather.

'Stand forth, alien,' said the machine voice. 'Let us get a better look at you.'

Saris glided forward, under the muzzles of guns. His lean brown form was crouched low, umoving save that the very end of his tail twitched hungrily. He watched the tank with cold eyes.

'Yes,' said the Thrymans after a long interval. 'Yes, there is something about him— We have never felt those particular life-currents before, in any of a hundred races. He may well be dangerous.'

'He'll be useful,' said Brannoch.

'If that effect *can* be duplicated mechanically, my lord,' interrupted Valti in his most oleaginous tone. 'Are you so sure of the possibility? Could it not be that *only* a living nervous system of his type can generate that field ... or control it? Control is a most complex problem, you know; it may require something as good as a genuine brain, which no known science has ever made artificially.'

'That is a matter for study,' mumbled Brannoch. 'It's up to the scientists.'

'And if your scientists fail? Has that eventuality occurred to you? Then you have precipitated a war without the advantage you were hoping for. Sol's forces *are* larger and better coördinated than yours, my lord. They might win an all-out victory.'

Langley had to admire the resolute way Brannoch faced an idea which had not existed for him before. He stood a while, looking down at his feet, clenching and unclenching his hands. 'I don't know,' he said at last, quietly. 'I'm not a scientist myself. What of it, Thrymka? Do you think it can be done?'

'The chance of the task being an impossible one has been considered by us,' answered the tank. 'It has a finite probability.'

'Well ... maybe the best thing to do is disintegrate him, then. We may be taking too much of a gamble – because I won't be able to fool Chanthavar very long. Perhaps we should stall, build up our conventional armaments for a few more years—'

'No,' said the monsters. 'The factors have been weighed. The optimum date for war is very near now, with or without the nullifier.'

'Are you sure?'

'Do not ask needless questions. You would lose weeks trying to understand the details of our analysis. Proceed as planned.'

'Well ... all right!' The decision made for him, Brannoch plunged into action as if eager to escape thought. He rapped out his orders, and the prisoners were marched off to a block of cells. Langley had a glimpse of Marin as she went by, then he and Saris were thrust together into one small room. A barred door clanged shut behind them, and two Thorians stood by their guns just outside.

The room was small and bare and windowless: sanitary facilities, a pair of bunks, nothing else. Langley sat down and gave Saris, who curled by his feet, a weary grin. 'This reminds me of the way the cops back in my time used to shift a suspect from one jail to another, keeping him a jump ahead of his lawyer and a habeas corpus writ.'

The Holatan did not ask for explanations; it was strange how relaxed he lay. After a while, Langley went on: 'I wonder why they stuck us in the same room.'

'Becausse we can together talk,' said Saris.

'Oh ... you sense recorders, microphones, in the wall? But we're talking English.'

'Doubtless they iss ... they hawe translation facilitiess. Our discussion iss recorded and iss translated tomorrow, maybe.'

'Hm-m-m, yeah, Well, there isn't anything important we can talk about anyway. Let's just think up remarks on Centaurian ancestry, appearance, and morals.'

'Oh, but we hawe much to discuss, my friend,' said Saris. 'I shall stop the recorder when we come to such topics.'

Langley laughed, a short hard bark. 'Good enough! And those birds outside don't savvy English.'

'I wish my t'oughtss to order,' said the Holatan. 'Meanwhile, see if you can draw them out in conwersation. Iss especially important to learn T'ryman motiwes.'

'So? I should think you'd be more interested to know what's going to become of you. They were talking about killing you back there, just in case you don't know.'

'Iss not so wital as you t'ink.' Saris closed his eyes.

Langley gave him a puzzled stare. *I'll never figure that critter out.* The flicker of hope was faintly astonishing; he suppressed it and strolled over to the door.

One of the guards swung up his gun, nervously. It had a nonstandard look about it: probably a smoothbore, designed and built for this one job, but no less dangerous. 'Take it easy, son,' said Langley. 'I don't bite . . . often.'

'We have strict orders,' said the Thorian. He was young, a little frightened, and it thickened the rough accent. 'If anything at all goes wrong, whether it seems to be your fault or not, you're both to be shot. Remember that.'

'Taking no chances, huh? Well, suit yourselves.' Langley leaned on the bars. It wasn't hard to act relaxed and companionable – not any more, now when nothing mattered. 'I was just wondering what you boys were getting out of it.'

'What do you mean?'

'Well, I suppose you came here along with the diplomatic mission, or maybe in a later consignment. When did you hit Earth?'

'Three years ago,' said the other guard. 'Outplanet service is normally for four.'

'But that don't include transportation time,' pointed out Langley. 'Makes about thirteen years you're gone. Your parents have gotten old, maybe died; your girl friend has married someone else . . . Back where I come from, we'd consider that a long term.'

'Shut up!' The answer was a bit too stiff and prompt.

'I'm not talking sedition,' said Langley mildly. 'Just wondering. Suppose you get paid pretty well, eh, to compensate?'

'There are bonuses for outplanet service,' said the first guard.

'Big ones?'

'Well—'

'I kind of thought so. Not enough to matter. The boys go off for a couple of decades; the old folks have to mortgage the farm to keep going; the boys come back without money to get out of hock, and spend the rest of their lives working for somebody else – some banker who was smart enough to stay at home. The rich get richer and the poor get poorer. Happened on Earth seven thousand years ago. Place called Rome.'

The heavy, blunt faces – faces of stolid, slow-thinking, stubborn yeomen – screwed up trying to find a suitably devastating retort; but nothing came out.

'I'm sorry,' said Langley. 'Didn't mean to needle you. I'm just curious, you see. Looks as if Centauri's going to be top dog, so I ought to learn about you, eh? I suppose you personally figure on getting a nice piece of land in the Solar System. But why is Thrym backing you?'

'Thrym is part of the League,' said one of the men. Langley didn't miss the reluctance in his tone. 'They go along with us . . . they simply have to.'

'But they have a vote, don't they? They could have argued against this adventure. Or have they been promised Jupiter to colonize?'

'They couldn't,' said the guard. 'Some difference in the air, not enough ammonia I think. They can't use any planet in this system.'

'Then why are they interested in conquering Sol? Why are they backing you? Sol never hurt them any, but Thor fought a war with them not so long ago.'

'They were beaten,' said the guard.

'Like hell they were, son. You can't beat a unified planet larger than all the others put together. The war was a draw, and you know it. The most Earth and Thor together could do, I'll bet, is mount guard on Thrym, keep the natives down there where they belong. Thor alone could only compromise, and take the short end of the stick at that. The Thrymans did win their point, you know; there aren't any human colonies on the Proximan planets.

'So I still wonder what Thrym's getting out of this deal.'

'I don't want to talk about it any longer!' said the guard angrily. 'Go on back.'

Langley stood for a moment, considering the situation. There were no soldiers in the cell block except these two. The door was held by an electronic lock, Saris could open it with a mere effort of will. But the two young men were keyed to an almost hysterical pitch; at the first sign of anything unforeseen, they'd open up on their prisoners. There didn't seem to be any way out of here.

He turned back to Saris. 'Got your thoughts uncoiled?' he asked.

'Somewhat.' The Holatan gave him a sleepy look. 'You may be astonished at certain t'ingss I hawe to say.'

'Go ahead.'

'I cannot read the human mind – not its actual t'oughtss, only its pressence and its emotional state. Giwen time, I could learn to do more, but there iss not been time yet, ewen wit' you. But the T'rymanss hawe a very long time had to study your race.'

'So they can read our thoughts, eh? Hm-m-m – bet Chant-havar doesn't know that! Then that inspection here they mentioned would have been via the superintendent's mind, I suppose – But are you sure?'

'Yess. It iss a certainty. Let me explain.'

The exposition was short and to the point. Every living nervous system radiates energy of several kinds. There are the electrical impulses, which encephalography had discovered in man even before Langley's time; there is a little heat; there is the subtler and more penetrating emission in the gyromagnetic spectrum. But the pattern varies: each race has its own norms. An encephalographer from Earth would not find the alpha rhythm of the human brain in a Holatan; he would have to learn a whole new 'language'.

On most planets, including Earth, there is little or no sensitivity to such emissions. The evolving life develops reactions to such vibrations as light and sound and, these being sufficient for survival purposes, does not go on to an ability to 'listen in' on nervous impulses. Except for a few dubious freaks – to this day, the subject of ESP in man was one for debate and bafflement – humanity is telepathically deaf. But on some planets, through a statistically improbable series of mutations, ESP organs do develop and most animals have them: including the intelligent animals, if any. In the case of Holat, the development was unique – the animal could not only receive the nervous impulses of others, but could at short range induce them. This was the basis of Holatan emotional empathy; it was also the reason Saris could control a vacuum tube. As if following some law of compensation, the perceptive faculty was poor on the verbal level; the Holatans used sonic speech because they could not get clear ideas across telepathically.

Thryman telepathy was of the 'normal' sort – the monsters could listen in, but could not influence, except via the specialized nerve endings in their joined feelers.

But a telepathic listener does not perceive pure thought. 'Thought' does not exist as part of the real world; there is only the process of *thinking*, the flow of pulses across synapses. The Thryman did not read a man's mind as such, but read the patterns of subvocalization. A man thinking on the conscious level 'talks to himself': the motor impulses go from brain to throat as if he were speaking aloud, but are suppressed en route. It was these impulses that the Thryman sensed and interpreted.

So to read the thoughts of another being, they had to know that being's language first. And Saris and Langley habitually thought in languages unknown to them. What they detected was gibberish.

'I . . . see.' The man nodded. 'It makes sense. I read about a case once which happened some hundred years before my time. An alleged telepath was demonstrating before the Pope – that was a religious person back then. He got confused, said he couldn't understand, and the Pope answered he'd been thinking in Latin. Yes, that may have been the same thing.' He smiled, grimly. 'Keeping our mental privacy is one consolation, at least.'

'There iss otherss,' replied the Holatan. 'I hawe a warning to giwe you. There iss soon to be an attack.'

'*Huh?*'

'Act not so alarmed. But the female you hawe – Marin iss her name? In her I hawe detected an electronic circuit.'

'What?' Langley sucked in his breath. There was an eerie tingle along his nerves. 'But . . . that's impossible . . . she—'

'In her iss been planted surgically a t'ing which I t'ink iss a wariable-frequency emitter. She can be traced. I would hawe told Walti, but wass not then familiar wit' the human nerwous system. I t'ought it a normal pattern for your femaless, ewen ass ours iss different from the maless. But now that I hawe seen more of you, I realize the trut'.'

Langley felt himself shivering. Marin – Marin again! But how—?

Then he understood. The time she had been seized, and returned. It had been for a purpose, after all; he, Langley, had not been the goal of that raid. An automatic communicator similar to Valti's, planted in her body by today's surgery – yes.

And such a device would be short-range, which meant that only a system of detectors spotted around the planet could hope to follow her. And only Chanthavar could have such a system.

Langley groaned: 'How many people's Judas goat is she, anyway?'

'We must be prepared,' said the Holatan calmly. 'Our guards will try to kill us in case of such, no? Forewarned, we may be able to—'

'Or to warn Brannoch?' Langley played with the idea a minute but discarded it. No. Even if the Centaurians got clean away, Sol's battle fleet would be on their heels; the war, the empty useless crazy war, would be started like an avalanche.

Let Chanthavar win, then. It didn't matter.

Langley buried his face in his hands. Why keep on fighting? Let him take his lead like a gentleman when the raid came.

No. Somehow, he felt he must go on living. He had been given a voice, however feeble, in today's history; it was up to him to keep talking as long as possible.

It might have been an hour later that Saris' muzzle nosed him to alertness. 'Grawity wibrationss. I t'ink the time iss now.'

CHAPTER SIXTEEN

A SIREN hooted. As its echoes rang down the hall, the guards jerked about, frozen for a bare instant.

The door flew open and Saris Hronna was through. His tigerish leap smashed one man into the farther wall. The other went spinning, to fall a yard away. He was still gripping his weapon. He bounced to his feet, raising it, as Langley charged him.

The spaceman was not a boxer or wrestler. He got hold of the gun barrel, twisting it aside, and sent his other fist in a right cross to the jaw. The Thorian blinked, spat blood, but failed to collapse. Instead, he slammed a booted kick at Langley's ankle. The American lurched away, pain like a lance in him. The Centaurian backed, lifting the musket. Saris brushed Langley aside in a single bound and flattened the man.

'Iss you well?' he asked, wheeling about. 'Iss hurt?'

'I'm still moving.' Langley shook his head, tasting the acridness of defeat. 'Come on . . . spring the rest. Maybe we can still make a break during the fracas.'

Shots and explosions crashed through the other rooms. Valti stumbled forth, his untidy red head lowered bull-like. 'This way!' he roared. 'Follow me! There must be a rear exit.'

The prisoners crowded after him, swiftly down the corridor to a door which Saris opened. A ramp led upward to ground level. Saris hunched himself – anything might be waiting beyond. But there was no alternative. The camouflaged entrance flew up for him, and he bounded into a late daylight.

Black patrol ships swarmed overhead like angry bees. There was a flier near one of the buildings. Saris went after it in huge leaps. He was almost there when a blue-white beam from the sky slashed it in half.

Wheeling with a snarl, the Holatan seemed to brace himself. A police vessel suddenly reeled and crashed into another. They fell in flame. Saris sprang for the edge of the compound, the humans gasping in his wake. A curtain of fire dropped over his path. Valti shouted something, pointing behind, and they saw black-clad slave soldiers rushing from the underground section.

'Stop their weapons!' shrieked Langley. He had one of the muskets, he laid it to his cheek and fired. The crack of it and the live recoil were a glory to him. A man spun on his heel and fell.

'Too many.' Saris lay down on the bare earth, panting. 'Iss more than I can handle. I had little hope for escape anyhow.'

Langley threw down his gun, cursing the day of creation.

The corpsmen ringed them in, warily. 'Sirs, you are all under arrest,' said the leader. 'Please accompany us.'

Marin wept, quietly and brokenly, as she followed them.

Chanthavar was in the plantation office. The walls were ringed with guards, and Brannoch stood gloomily to one side. The Solarian was immaculate, and his cheerfulness hardly showed at all.

'How do you do, Captain Langley,' he said. 'And Goltam Valti, sir, of course. Well, gentlemen, I seem to have arrived in the well-known nick of time.'

'Go ahead,' said the spaceman. 'Shoot us and get it over with.'

Chanthavar raised his brows. 'Why such a flair for drama?' he asked.

An officer entered, bowed, and reeled off his report. The hideaway was taken, all personnel dead or under arrest, our casualties six killed and ten wounded. Chanthavar gave an order, and Saris was herded into a specially prepared cage and borne outside.

'In case you're wondering, captain,' said the agent, 'the way I found you was—'

'I know,' said the spaceman.

'Oh? Oh . . . yes, of course. Saris would have detected it. I was gambling there; didn't think he'd realize in time what it was, and apparently he didn't. There were other tracing procedures in readiness, this happens to be the one which worked.' Chanthavar's lips curved into his peculiarly engaging smile. 'No grudges, captain. You tried to do what seemed best, I'm sure.'

'How about us?' rumbled Brannoch.

'Well, my lord, the case clearly calls for deportation.'

'All right. Let us go. I have a ship.'

'Oh, no, my lord. We couldn't be so discourteous. The Technate will prepare transportation for you. It may take a while – even a few months—'

'Till you get a head start on the nullifier research. I see.'

'Meanwhile, you and your staff will kindly remain in your own quarters. I shall post guards to see that you are not . . . disturbed.'

'All right.' Brannoch forced his mouth into a sour grin. 'I

have to thank you for that, I suppose. In your position, I'd have shot me down out of hand.'

'Some day, my lord, your death may be necessary,' said Chanthavar. 'At present, though, I owe you something. This affair is going to mean a good deal to my own position, you understand – there are higher offices than my present one, and they will soon be open for me.'

He turned back to Langley. 'I've already made arrangements for you, captain. Your services won't be required any longer; we have found a couple of scholars who can talk Old American, and between them and the hypnotic machines Saris can be given a near-perfect command of the modern language in a few days. As for you, a position and an apartment at the university in Lora has been fixed up. The historians, archeologists, and planetographers are quite anxious to consult you. The pay is small, but you'll keep free-born rank.'

Langley said nothing. So he was to be taken out of the game already. That was the end – back in the box with you, my pawn.

Valti cleared his throat. 'My lord,' he said pompously, 'I must remind you that the Society—'

Chanthavar gave him a long stare through narrowed eyes. The smooth face had gone utterly expressionless. 'You have committed criminal acts within the laws of Sol,' he said.

'Extraterritoriality—'

'It doesn't apply here. At best, you can be deported.' Chanthavar seemed to brace himself. 'Nevertheless, I am letting you go free. Get your men together, take one of the plantation fliers, and go on back to Lora.'

'My lord is most gracious,' said Valti. 'May I ask why?'

'Never mind why. Get out.'

'My lord, I am a criminal. I confess it. I want a fair trial by a mixed tribunal as provided in Article VIII, Section 4, of the Treaty of Lunar.'

Chanthavar's eyes were flat and cold. 'Get out or I'll have you thrown out.'

'I demand to be arrested!' shouted Valti. 'I insist on my right and privilege of clearing my own conscience. If you won't book me, I shall complain directly to the Technon.'

'Very well!' Chanthavar spat it out. 'I have orders from the Technon itself to let you go scot-free. Why, I don't know. But it's an order; it came as soon as I filed report of the situation and of my intention to attack. Are you satisfied?'

'Yes, my lord,' said Valti blandly. 'Thank you for your kindness. Good day, gentlemen.' He bowed clumsily and stumped out.

Chanthavar broke into a laugh. 'Insolent old beetle! I didn't want to tell him, but he'd have learned it anyway in time. Now let him wonder along with the rest of us. The Technon gets mysterious now and then – a brain planning a thousand years ahead has to, I suppose.' He rose and stretched. 'Let's go. Maybe I can still make that concert at Salma tonight.'

Langley blinked at the sunshine outside. The tropics of Earth had gotten still hotter in five thousand years. He saw a group of armed men boarding a military flier, and there was a sudden wrenching in his heart.

'Chanthavar,' he asked, 'can I say good-by to Saris?'

'I'm sorry.' The agent shook his head, not without compassion. 'I know he's your friend, but there have been too many risks taken in this business already.'

'Well . . . will I ever see him again?'

'Perhaps. We aren't brutes, captain. We don't intend to mistreat him if he coöperates.' Chanthavar waved to a smaller machine. 'I think that's yours. Good-by, captain. I hope to see you again sometime if I get the chance.' He turned and strode briskly off. The dust scuffed up under his buskins.

Langley and Marin entered the flier. One silent guard went along; he set the autopilot, they rose smoothly, and he sat down in front of them to wait with drilled patience.

The girl was mute for a long while. 'How did they find us?' she asked at last.

The spaceman told her.

She didn't cry this time. There seemed to be no tears left. They said almost nothing during the hour of bulleting homeward flight.

Lora raised over a nighted horizon, like one huge fountain of soaring metal pride. The flier buzzed around, finding a ledge on one of the smaller towers on the north side. The guard nodded. 'Your apartment is No. 337, right down the hall, sir,' he stated. 'Good evening.'

Langley led the way. When the door opened for him, he saw a layout of four small rooms, comfortable but unostentatious. There was a service robot, but clearly his new position did not include live slaves.

Except –

He faced around to Marin, and stood looking at her for a minute. She returned his gaze steadily, but she was pale and there was a darkness in her eyes. This blanched creature was not Peggy, he thought.

The rage and bitterness rose in his throat like vomit. All over. *C'est fini.* Here ends the saga. He had tried, and all his hopes had been kicked down, and *she* was the one who had wrecked them!

'Get out,' he said.

She lifted a hand to her mouth, as if he had struck her, but no words would come.

'You heard me.' He walked over the floor, it yielded ever so little as if it were of rubbery flesh, and stared through the window. 'I'm giving you your freedom. You're not a slave now. Understand?'

She made no reply, not yet.

'Are there any formalities involved?' he asked.

She told him. There was no life in her voice. He dialed the
records office and filed notice that he, sole owner of chattel
slave No. Such-and-such, was hereby emancipating her.
Then he turned, but he couldn't quite meet the green eyes.

'It wasn't your fault,' he said thickly. There was a thundering in his temples, and his legs wobbled under him. 'It
wasn't anybody's fault, we're all poor little victims of cir-
cumstance, and I've had enough of that line. You were just a
helpless tool, sure, I'm not condemning you. Nevertheless, I
can't stand having you around any longer. There's too much
failure in you. You have to go.'

'I'm sorry,' she whispered.

'So am I,' he said insincerely. 'Go on . . . get out . . . make
something of yourself.' With a barely conscious impulse, he
unfastened his purse and threw it at her. 'There. Good bit of
money in that. Take it – use it to establish yourself.'

She looked at him with a bewilderment which slowly
cleared. 'Good-by,' she said. Her back was straight as she
walked out. It wasn't till much later that he noticed she'd
left his purse where it fell.

CHAPTER SEVENTEEN

TOMORROW and tomorrow and tomorrow. This is the way
the world ends.

They were quiet, pleasant men in the university, they had
grave good manners but little formality and they were con-
siderate of the man from the past. Langley recalled his own
college days – he'd been a graduate assistant for a while and
had seen a bit of faculty life. Here there was none of the
gossip and small intrigue and hypocritical teas he remembered; but neither was there any spirit of eagerness and in-

tellectual adventure. Everything was known, everything settled and assured, it remained only to fill in the details. Back in the Twenty-first Century, masters' theses about the commas in Shakespeare had still been a subject for humor — today, the equivalent was a matter of course.

The library was magnificent and astonishing: a billion volumes reduced to magnetic patterns, any of them instantly located and copied by pressing a few buttons. The robots would even do your reading for you and make summaries, they would draw conclusions if you wanted them to: logical deductions with no hint of speculative imagination. The professors — they were called by a title which meant, roughly, 'repository of information' — were mostly of commoner stock, a few petty aristocrats, all selected by tests which made no allowance for birth. The rules of their order kept them strictly out of politics. There were only a few students, some dilettantes and some earnest youngsters intending to become professors in their turn. The sons of Ministers went from private tutors to special academies; the university was a dying vestige of an earlier period, maintained simply because the Technon had not ordered its abolition.

Nevertheless, Langley found these graying, brown-robed men congenial company. There was one historian in particular, a little wizened man with a huge bald head, Jant Mardos, with whom he got quite friendly: the chap had enormous crudition and a refreshingly sardonic viewpoint. They used to spend hours talking, while a recorder took down everything which was said for later evaluation.

For Langley, it was the nights which were worst.

'. . . The present situation was, of course, inevitable,' said Mardos. 'If a society is not to petrify, it must innovate, as yours did; but sooner or later a point is reached at which further innovation becomes impractical, and then petrifaction sets in anyway. For example, the unification of Earth was necessary if man was to survive, but in time that unification destroyed the cultural variety and interplay which had been responsible for much progress up to then.'

'Seems to me you could still make changes,' said the spaceman, 'Political changes, at least.'

'What sort? You might as well face it, the Technon is the best possible device for government – if we wrecked it, we'd go back to corruption, incompetence, and internecine strife. We have those already, of course, but they don't matter very much, since policy is decided by a machine which is able, incorruptible, and immortal.'

'Still, why not give the Commoners a break? Why should they have to spend their lives down on low-level?'

Mardos raised his brows. 'My dear romantic friend, what else can they do? Do you think they're fit to share administrative responsibilities? The average IQ of the Commons is about 90, the average for the Ministerial class is closer to 150.' He laid his fingertips carefully together. 'To be sure, by automatizing all operations, it would be possible for every man in the Solar System to quit work: all his needs would be supplied free. But what, then, is your IQ-90 Commoner going to do with himself? Play chess and write epic poems?

'Even as things are, there isn't enough work to go around for the Ministers. That's why you see so many wastrels and so much politicking among them.

'Let's admit it: man in the known universe has exhausted the possibilities of his own culture. You wouldn't expect them to be infinite, after all. There are only so many shapes into which you can carve a block of marble; once the sculptors have made the best ones, their successors face a choice between dull imitation and puerile experiment. The same applies to all the arts, the sciences, and the permutations of human relationships. As for politics, our civilization today may be ossified, but it is at least stable, and the majority are content that it remain so. For the ordinary man, instability –

change – means dislocation, war, uncertainty, misery, and death.'

Langley shook his head. 'The universe is bigger than we are,' he said. 'We can always find something new out there, always make a fresh start.'

'Are you thinking of the lost colonies?' asked Mardos. He snorted. 'Several bales of romantic nonsense have been written about them. But they were only people who couldn't make the grade at home and tried to escape. I doubt if they did any better out there.'

'You're pretty far from your own colonial period,' said Langley. 'In my time, though, we were still close to ours. I have a notion that progress, the new outlook on life, the fresh start, is mostly due to those same failures.'

'So?' Mardos pricked up his ears. 'What basis?'

'Oh ... all the history I know. Take Iceland; I had a friend from there who explained it to me. The first colonists were big men, even petty kings of a sort, who got kicked out of Norway when it was unified because they wouldn't knuckle under. They founded what was just about the first republic since Greek times; they wrote down some of the finest literature in the world; they made good tries at colonizing Greenland and America.

'Then the Americans themselves, my own people. Some of them were religious dissenters who couldn't get along with the churches at home. Some of them were deported criminals. The later immigrants were mostly impoverished bums, some few liberals who didn't like what was happening in Europe. And yet this bunch of malcontents and Commoners took over half a continent, gave republican government its first real start, led the parade in creating industry and technology, and grabbed the leadership in world affairs ... no, wait, they didn't grab it, didn't really want it, but they had it thrust on them because nobody else could hold that particular potato.

'Then there were the early interplanetary colonies, which I saw with my own eyes. The personnel weren't exactly fugitives, they were planted there, but they were the sort who fitted best into the new environment and got quite unhappy if you sent them back to Earth. The average intelligence was pretty terriffic.'

'You might be right,' said Mardos thoughtfully. 'Perhaps some few of the lost colonies have found a better way. For instance, if a shipload of really high-caliber people went off, no morons to drag them down—'

'And most rebels are high-caliber,' put in Langley. 'They wouldn't be rebels if they were dumb enough and spineless enough to accept things as they are.'

'Well, who wants to spend perhaps thousands of years external time looking for them? That's sheer escapism.'

'I've got a hunch that history is made by that kind of escapist.'

'The Commercial Society has ranged for hundreds of light-years and found nothing like what you dream of.'

'Certainly not. A group which wanted to get away from what it considered an evil civilization would go further than that. And there's the idea of something hid behind the ranges—'

'Immature!'

'Of course. Don't forget, the immature human – or society – is in process of growing up. But speaking of *the* Society, I'd like to know more about it. I've got a kind of suspicion—'

'There isn't a great deal of information. They've been pretty secretive. They seem to have originated right here on Earth, a thousand or so years ago, but the history is obscure.'

'It shouldn't be,' said Langley. 'Isn't the Technon supposed to keep complete records of everything important? And surely the Society is important – anyone could have foreseen they'd become a major factor.'

'Go ahead,' shrugged Mardos. 'You can use the library as much as will amuse you.'

Langley found himself a desk and asked for a bibliography. It was surprisingly small. By way of comparison, he got a reference list for Tau Ceti IV, a dreary little planet of no special value – it was several times as long as the first.

He sat for some minutes meditating on the effects of a static culture. To him, the paucity of information fairly screamed *Cover-up*. But these so-called savants around him merely noted that few books and articles were available, and proceeded to forget all about the subject.

He plunged doggedly into the task of reading everything he could find on the topic. Economic statistics; cases where the Society had interfered in local politics on one or another planet, to protect itself; discourses on the psychology produced by a lifetime aboard ship – and an item dated one thousand, ninety-seven years ago, to the effect that one Hardis Sanj, representing a group of interstellar traders – list of names attached – had applied for a special charter and that this had been granted. Langley read the charter; it was a sweeping document, its innocuous language gave powers which a Minister might envy. Three hundred years later, the Technon entered a recognition of the Society as an independent state; other planets had already done so, the rest soon followed suit. Since then there had been treaties and—

Langley sat very still, four days after his research had begun. It added up.

Item: The Technon had let the Society go without any argument, though otherwise its basic policy was frankly aimed at the gradual re-unification of the accessible galaxy.

Item: The Society had several hundred million members by now, including personnel from many nonhuman races.

No one member of it knew more than a fraction of the others.

Item: The rank and file of the Society, up through ships' officers, did not know who their ultimate rulers were, but had been conditioned to obedience and a strange lack of curiosity about them.

Item: the Technon itself had ordered Chanthavar to release Valti without prejudice.

Item: The economic data showed that over long periods of time, more and more planets were becoming dependent on the Society for one or another vital element of their industry. It was easier and cheaper to trade with the nomads than to go out and get it for yourself: and the Society was, after all, quite neutral—

Like hell!

Langley wondered why no one else seemed to suspect the truth. Chanthavar, now – But Chanthavar, however intelligent, was conditioned too; his job was merely to carry out policy set by the machine, not to inquire deeply. Of course no Minister could be permitted to know – such as did, from time to time, stumble on the facts, would disappear. Because if any unauthorized person found out, the secret could not be kept, it would soon be spread between the stars and the Society's usefulness would end.

Its usefulness to the Technon.

Of course! The Society was founded soon after the colonies had broken away. There was no hope of taking them over again in the foreseeable future. But a power which went everywhere and filed reports for an unknown central office – a power which everybody, including its own membership, believed to be disinterested and unaggressive – there was the perfect agent for watching and gradually dominating the other planets.

What a machine the Technon must be! What a magnificent monument, supreme final achievement of an aging science! Its creators had wrought better than they knew; their child grew up, became capable of thinking millennia ahead, until at last it *was* civilization. Langley had a sudden, irrational wish to see that enormous engine; but it could never be.

Was that thing of metal and energy really a conscious brain? No ... Valti had said, and the library confirmed, that the living mind in all its near-infinite capacities had never been artificially duplicated. That the Technon thought, reasoned, within the limits of its own function, could not be doubted. Some equivalent of creative imagination was needed to run whole planets and to devise schemes like the Society. But it was still a robot, a super-computer; its decisions were still made strictly on the basis of data given it, and would be erroneous to the same degree that the data were.

A child – a great, nearly omnipotent, humorless child, fixing the destiny of a race which had abdicated its own responsibilities. The thought was not cheerful.

Langley struck a cigarette and leaned back. All right. He'd made a discovery which could shake an empire. That was because he came from an altogether different age, with a different way of living and thinking. He had the unsubmissive intellect of the free-born without their mental blinkers; his world had a history of steady, often violent evolution behind it, had made an idol of 'progress', so he could observe today with more detachment than people who for the past two millennia had striven only for stasis.

But what to to with his facts?

He had a nihilistic desire to call up Valti and Chanthavar and tell them. Blow the whole works apart. But no – who was he to upset an apple cart holding billions of lives, and probably get himself killed in the process? He didn't have the judgment, he wasn't God – his wish was merely a reflex of impotent rage.

So I'd better just keep my mouth shut. If there was ever

any suspicion of what I've learned, I wouldn't last a minute.
I was important for a while, and look what happened.

Alone in his apartment that night, he regarded himself in a mirror. The face had grown thin and lost most of its tan. The gray streaks in his hair had spread. He felt very old and tired.

Regret nagged him. Why had he shot that man in the African compound? It had been a futile gesture, as futile as everything he tried in this foreign world. It had snuffed out a life – or, at least, given pain – for no purpose at all.

He simply didn't belong here.

'*She sat down beside me,*
And taking my hand,
Said: "You are a stranger,
And in a strange land."'

She! What was Marin doing? Was she even alive? Or could you call it life, down there on low-level? He didn't think she would sell herself, she'd starve to death first with the angry pride he knew, but anything could happen in the Old City.

Remorse clawed at him. He shouldn't have sent her away. He shouldn't have taken out his own failure on her, who had only wanted to share his burden. His present salary was small, hardly enough to support two, but they could have worked something out.

Blindly, he dialed the city's main police office. The courteous slave face told him that the law did not permit free tracing of a Commoner who was not wanted for some crime. A special service was available at a price of – more money than he had. Very sorry, sir.

Borrow the money. Steal it. Go down to low-level himself, offer rewards, anything, but find her!

And would she even want to come back?

Langley found himself trembling. 'This won't do, son,' he said aloud, into the emptiness of the room. 'You're going loco fast. Sit down and do some thinking for a change.'

But all his thoughts scurried through the same rat race. He was the outsider, the misfit, the square peg, existing only on charity and a mild intellectual interest. There was nothing he could do, he had no training, no background; if it hadn't been for the university, itself an anachronism, he would be down in the slums.

Some deep stubbornness in him forbade suicide. But its other aspect, insanity, was creeping after him. This sniveling self-pity was the first sign of his own disintegration.

How long had he been here at the university? About two weeks, and already he was caving in.

He told the window to open. There was no balcony, but he leaned out and breathed hard. The night air was warm and damp. Even this high, he could smell the miles of earth and growing plants. The stars wavered overhead, jeering at him with remoteness.

Something moved out there, a flitting shadow. It came near, and he saw dully that it was a man in a spacesuit, flying with a personal anti-gravity unit. Police model. Who were they after now?

The black armor swooped close. Langley jumped back as it came through the window. It landed with a thump that quivered in the floor.

'What the hell—' Langley stepped closer. One metal-gauntleted hand reached up, unfastened the blocky helmet, slapped it back. A huge nose poked from a tangle of red hair.

'Valti!'

'In the flesh,' said the trader. 'Quite a bit of flesh too, eh?' He polarized the window as he ordered it shut. 'How are you, captain? You look rather weary.'

'I . . . am.' Slowly, the spaceman felt his heartbeat pick up, and there was a tautness gathering along his nerves. 'What do you want?'

'A little chat, captain, merely a little private discussion. Fortunately, we do keep some regulation Solar equipment at the office – Chanthavar's men are getting infernally interested in our movements, it's hard to elude them. I trust we may talk undisturbed?'

'Ye-e-es. I think so. But—'

'No refreshment, thank you. I have to be gone as soon as possible. Things are starting to happen again.' Valti chuckled and rubbed his hands together. 'Yes, indeed. I knew the Society had tentacles in high places, but I never thought our influence was so great.'

'C-c-c—' Langley stopped, took a deep breath, and forced himself into a chilly calm. 'Get to the point, will you? What do you want?'

'To be sure. Captain, do you like it here? Have you quite abandoned your idea of making a new start elsewhere?'

'So I'm being offered that again. Why?'

'Ah . . . my chiefs have decided that Saris Hronna and the nullifier effect are not to be given up without a struggle. I have been ordered to have him removed from confinement. Believe it or not my orders were accompanied by authentic, uncounterfeitable credentials from the Technon. Obviously, we have some very clever agents high in the government of Sol, perhaps in the Servants corps. They were able to give the machine false data such that it automatically concluded its own best interests lay in getting Saris away from Chanthavar.'

Langley went over to the service robot and got a stiff drink. Only after he had it down did he trust himself to speak. 'And you need me,' he said.

'Yes, captain. The operation will be hazardous in all events. If Chanthavar finds out, he will naturally take it on himself to stop everything till he can question the Technon further – then, in the light of such fresh data, it will order an investigation and learn the truth. So we must act fast. You

will be needed as Saris' friend in whom he has confidence,
and the possessor of an unknown common language with
him – he must know ours already – so he will know what we
are about and coöperate with us.'

The Technon! Langley's brain spun. What fantastic new
scheme had that thing hatched now?

'I suppose,' he said slowly, 'we'll be going to Cygni first as
you originally planned.'

'No.' The plump face tightened, and there was the faintest
quaver in the voice. 'I don't really understand. We're supposed to turn him over to the Centaurians.'

CHAPTER EIGHTEEN

LANGLEY made no reply. There didn't seem to be anything
to say.

'I don't know why,' Valti told him. 'I often think that we,
the Society, must have a Technon of our own. The decisions
are sometimes incomprehensible to me, though they have
always worked out for the best. It means war if either side
gets the nullifier ... and why should the Centaurian barbarians get the advantage?'

'Why indeed?' whispered Langley. The night was utterly
still around him.

'I can only think that ... that Sol represents a long-
range menace to us. It is, after all, a rigid culture; if it
became dominant, it might act against us, who cannot
be fitted into its own static pattern. It's probably best in
the light of history that the Centaurians take over for a
while.'

'Yeah,' said Langley.

This tore it. This knocked everything he had thought into

a ten-gallon hat. Apparently the Technon was *not* the real
boss of the nomads. And yet –

'I tell you this in all honesty,' said Valti. 'It might have
been easier to keep you in ignorance, but that was a risk.
When you found out what we were up to, you and Saris
could make trouble between you. Best to get your free con-
sent at the start.

'For your own help, captain, you are offered a manned
spaceship in which you can find your own planet, if you
don't like any known to us. Nor need you worry about betraying Saris; he'll be no worse off on Thor than on Earth,
indeed you will be in a position to bargain and assure good
treatment for him. But I must have your decision now.'

Langley shook his head. This was too much, too suddenly. 'Let me think a bit. How about Brannoch's gang?
Have they been in touch with you?'

'No. I know only that we are supposed to get them out of
the embassy tower, where they are being kept under house
arrest, and provide transportation to Thor for them. I have
papers from the Technon which will get us in there too, if we
use them right.'

'Haven't they contacted anybody?'

It couldn't be seen through the rigid spacesuit, but Valti
must have shrugged. 'Officially, no. Certainly not us. But in
practice, of course, the Thrymans must have variable-frequency communicators secreted in their tank, where human
police could hardly go to search. They must have been talking to their agents on Earth by that means, though what was
said I don't know. Chanthavar realizes as much, but there's
little he can do about it except to have the Thrymans destroyed, and that goes against the gentlemanly code. These
high-ranking lords of different states respect each other's
rights ... they never know when they might find themselves in the same fix.'

'So.' Langley stood immobile, but the knowledge was
rising in him and he wanted to shout it.

He hadn't been wrong. The Technon did rule the Society. But there was, there must be, an additional complication, and he thought he had grasped its nature.

'I ask you again, captain,' said Valti. 'Will you help?'

'If not,' said the spaceman dryly, 'I suppose your disappointment would be quite violent.'

'I would infinitely regret it,' murmured Valti, touching the blaster at his side. 'But some secrets are rather important.' His small pale eyes studied the other. 'I will, however, accept your word if you do agree to help. You're that kind of man. Also, you could gain little or nothing by betraying us.'

Langley made his decision. It was a leap into darkness, but suddenly he felt calm rising within himself, an assurance which was like a steadying hand. He was going somewhere again – it might only be over a precipice, but he was out of the maze and walking like a man.

'Yes,' he said. 'I'll come along. '*If*.'

Valti waited.

'Same terms as before. The girl Marin is to accompany us. Only first I've got to find her. She's been manumitted – down on low-level somewhere. When she's back here, I'll be ready to leave.'

'Captain, it may take days to—'

'That's too bad. Give me a fistful of money and I'll make a stab at locating her myself.'

'The operation is set for tomorrow night. Can you do it by then?'

'I think so – given enough money.'

Valti emitted a piteous groan, but dug deep. It was a very fat purse which Langley clipped to his belt. He also held out for a small blaster, which he holstered beneath his cloak.

'Very well, captain,' said the trader. 'Good luck. I'll expect you to be in the Twin Moons at 2100 hours tomorrow night. If not—'

'I know.' Langley drew a finger across his throat. 'I'll be
there.'

Valti bowed, lowered his helmet, and left the same way he
had come.

Langley could have wept and howled for sheer excitement, but there wasn't time. He went out of the apartment
and down the halls. They were deserted at this hour. The
bridgeway beyond was still jammed, but when he took a
grav-shaft going down he was alone.

It brawled and shouted in the Commons, crowds milled
about him, in his drab university gown he met little respect
and had to push his way. Down to Etie Town.

It lay on the border of the slum section, but was itself
orderly and well policed. There were some humans living in
or near it, he knew, hired help. A nonhuman had no interest
in a woman, except as a servant. It would be the safest place
for a girl thrown out of high-level to go. At least, it was the
logical place to begin his search.

He had been a clumsy amateur, grown mentally paralyzed
by his own repeated failures in a world of professionals.
That feeling was gone now. The magnitude of his deter-
mination lent an assurance which was almost frightening.
This time nothing was going to get in his way without being
trampled down!

He entered a tavern. Its customers were mostly of a scaly,
bi-pedal race with snouted heads, who didn't need special
conditions of atmosphere or temperature. They ignored
him as he walked through the weird maze of wet sponge
couches they favored. The light was dull red, hard to see
by.

Langley went over to a corner where a few men in the
livery of paid servants were drinking. They stared at him, it
must be the first time a professor had come in here. 'May I
sit down?' he asked.

'Kind of crowded,' snapped a sulky-looking man.

'Sorry. I was going to buy a round, but—'

'Oh, well, then, sit.'

Langley didn't mind the somewhat constrained silence that fell. It suited him perfectly. 'I'm looking for a woman,' he said.

'Four doors down.'

'No . . . a particular woman. Tall, dark red hair, upper-level accent. I think she must have come here about two weeks ago. Has anyone seen her?'

'No.'

'I'm offering a reward for the information. A hundred solars.'

Their eyes widened. Langley saw avarice on some of the faces, and flipped his cloak back in a casual way to reveal his gun. Its possession was a serious offense, but nobody seemed inclined to cry out for the police. 'Well, if you can't help me I'll just have to try somewhere else.'

'No . . . wait a minute, sir. Take it easy. Maybe we can.' The sulky man looked around the table. 'Anybody know her? No? It could be inquired about, though.'

'Sure.' Langley peeled off ten ten-solar notes. 'That's to hire inquirers. The reward is extra. But it's no good if she isn't found inside . . . Hm-m-m . . . three hours.'

His company evaporated. He sat down, ordered another drink, and tried to control his impatience.

Time dragged. How much of life went in simply waiting!

A girl came up with a suggestion. Langley sent her off to look too. He nursed his beers: now, as never before, he had to have a clear head.

In two hours and eighteen minutes, a breathless little man panted back to the table. 'I've found her!'

Langley's heart jumped. He stood up, taking it slow. 'Seen her?'

'Well, no. But a new maid answering her description did hire out to a Slimer – a merchant from Srinis, I mean – just

eleven days ago. The cook told me that, after somebody else
had tracked down the cook for me.'

The spaceman nodded. His guess had been right: the servant class would still know more gossip than a regiment of
police could track down. People hadn't changed so much.
'Let's go,' he said, and went out the door.

'How about my reward?'

'You'll get it when I see her. Control your emotions.'

Five thousand years ago, a bibliophile acquaintance had
made him read a tattered book some hundred years old – the
Private Eye school – claiming it was something unique in
the annals of pornography. Langley had been rather bored
by it. Now, recognizing the prototype of his action-pattern,
he grinned. But any pattern would do, in this amorphous
world of low-level.

They went down a broad street full of strangeness. The
little man stopped outside a door. 'This is the place. I don't
know how we get in, though.'

Langley punched the scanner button. Presently the door
opened, to reveal a human butler of formidable proportions.
The American was quite prepared to slug a way past him if
necessary. But he wasn't a slave – aliens weren't permitted
to own humans. He had been hired once, and could probably be hired again.

'Excuse me,' said Langley. 'Do you have a new maid, a
tall red-head?'

'Sir, my employer values his privacy.'

Langley ruffled a sheaf of large bills. 'Too bad. It's worth
a good deal to me. I only want to talk with her.'

He got in, leaving his informant to jitter outside. The air
was thick and damp, the light a flooding greenish yellow
which hurt his eyes. The outworlders would employ live servants for prestige, but must have to pay rather well. The
thought that he had driven Marin to this artificial swamp
was like teeth in his soul.

She stood in a chamber full of mist. Droplets of fog had condensed to glitter in her hair. Unsurprised eyes watched him gravely.

'I've come,' he whispered.

'I knew you would.'

'I'm . . . can I say how sorry I am?'

'You needn't, Edwy. Forget it.'

They returned to the street. Langley paid off his inform-ant and got the address of a hotel. He walked there, holding her hand, but said nothing till they were safely alone.

Then he kissed her, half afraid that she would recoil from him. But she responded with a sudden hunger. 'I love you,' he said; it was a new and surprising knowledge.

She smiled. 'That makes it mutual, I think.'

Later, he told her what had happened. It was like turn-ing on a light behind her eyes. 'And we can get away?' she asked softly. 'We can really start over? If you knew how I've dreamed of that, ever since—'

'Not so fast.' The grimness was returning, it put an edge in his voice and he twisted his fingers nervously. 'This is a pretty complicated situation. I think I know what's behind it – maybe you can help fill in the gaps.

'I've proven to myself that the Technon founded the Society and uses it as a spy and an agent of economic infiltration. *However* – the Technon is stuck away in a cave somewhere. It can't go out and supervise affairs; it has to rely on information supplied by its agents. Some of these agents are official, part of the Solar government; some of them are semiofficial, members of the Society; some are highly unofficial, spies on other planets.

'But two can play at the same game, you know. There's another race around which has a mentality much like the Technon's – a cold, impersonal mass-mind, planning cen-turies ahead, able to wait indefinitely long for some little seed to sprout. And that's the race on Thrym. Their mental hookup practice makes them that kind: an individual doesn't matter, because in a very real sense each individual is only a cell in one huge unit. You can see it operating in a case like the League, where they've quietly taken over the key position, made themselves boss so gradually that the Thorians hardly realize it even today.'

'And you think they have infiltrated the Society?' she asked.

'I know they have. There's no other answer. The Society wouldn't be turning Saris over to Brannoch if it were truly independent. Valti tried hard to rationalize it, but I know more than he does. I know the Technon thinks it still owns the Society, and that it'd never give Centauri an advantage.'

'But it has, you say,' she protested.

'Uh-huh. Here's the explanation as I see it. The Society includes a lot of races. One of those races is Thryman. Probably they're not officially from Thrym. They could have been planted on a similar world, maybe with some slight surgical changes in their appearance, and passed themselves off as natives. They got members into the nomad bureaucracy by the normal process of promotion and, being very able, eventually these members got high enough to learn the truth – that the Technon was behind the whole show.

'What a windfall for them! They must have infiltrated the Society on general principles, to get control of still another human group, but found they'd also gotten a line into the Technon itself. They can doctor the reports it gets from the Society – not every report, but enough. That power has to be saved for special occasions, because the machine must have data-comparison units, it must be capable of "suspicion", to do its job. This is a special occasion.

'Chanthavar, Brannoch, and Valti were all acting at cross purposes because there hadn't been time to consult the Technon; otherwise it would normally have told Valti to keep hands off the affair, or at least to coöperate with Chanthavar. When it was informed, you know, it ordered Valti's release.

'But then the Thrymans got busy. Even imprisoned, they must have been in touch with their agents outside, including high-ranking Thrymans in the Society.

'I don't know exactly what story has been fed the Technon. At a guess. I'd suggest something like this: A trading ship has just come back with news of a new planet inhabited by a race having Saris' abilities. They were studied, and it turned out that there is no way to duplicate that nullifying effect artificially. The Thrymans are perfectly capable of cooking up such a report complete with quantitative data and mathematical theory, I'll bet.

'All right. This report, supposedly from its own good, reliable Society, reaches the Technon. It makes a very natural decision: let the Centaurians have Saris, let them waste their time investigating a blind alley. It has to look real, so that Brannoch won't suspect; therefore, work through Valti without informing Chanthavar.

'So ... the end result is that Centauri does get the nullifier! And the first news the Technon has of this is when the invading fleet arrives able to put every ship in the Solar System out of action!'

Marin made no reply for a while. Then she nodded. 'That sounds logical,' she said. 'I remember now ... when I was at Brannoch's, just before coming to you, he spoke with that tank, mentioned something about Valti being troublesome and ripe for assassination, and the tank forbade him to do it. Shall we tell Chanthavar?'

'No,' said Langley.

'But do you want the Centaurians to win?'

'Emphatically not. I don't want a war at all, and letting this information out prematurely would be a sure way to start one. Can't you see the wild scramble to cover up, purge, strike at once lest you be further subverted?

'The fact that Brannoch himself is in the dark, that he knows nothing about this supremely important Society business, indicates to me that Thrym doesn't exactly have the interests of the League at heart either. The League is only a means to a much bigger and deadlier end.'

He lifted his head. 'So far, darling, my attempts to sit in on this game have been pretty miserable flops. I'm risking both our lives against what I think is the future of the human race. It sounds rather silly, doesn't it? One little man thinking he can change history all by his lonesome. A lot of trouble has been caused by that delusion.

'I'm gambling that this time, for once, it's not a mistake – that I really can carry off something worth while. Do you think I'm right? Do you think I even have a right to try?'

She came to him and laid her cheek against his. 'Yes,' she whispered. 'Yes, my dearest.'

CHAPTER NINETEEN

LANGLEY didn't exactly smuggle Marin back to his apartment – if she were noticed, it wouldn't excite much comment – but he did try to be discreet about it. Then he surprised himself by sleeping better than he had done for weeks.

On the following day, he took microcopies of all the library data on the Society, as well as having the robot prepare a summary, and stuck the spool in his purse. It was dismaying to reflect what a series of thin links his hopes depended on. Valti's character was one; he *thought* the trader could shake off a lifetime's conditioning enough to look a few facts and a little reasoning in the face, but was he sure?

Mardos had him in for another interview. The historian

was getting eager, as one unknown datum after another emerged. Some of his careful cynicism dropped off: 'Think of it! The very dawn of the technological and space-travel era – the most crucial epoch since man invented agriculture – and you lived in it! You know, you've already upset a dozen well-established theories. We had no idea that there was so much cultural difference between nations, then, for instance. It explains a good many puzzling features of later history.'

'So you'll write a book?' asked Langley. He was having a hard time keeping up the act, it was all he could do not to pace the floor and chain-smoke as he waited for evening.

'Oh, yes . . . yes.' Mardos got a shy look on his face. 'And yet . . . well, I started out with the notion that I might get some small fame and an upgrading out of this. Now I don't care. It's only the job itself, the learning, that matters. You . . . you've shown me a little of what it must have been like in your age, the feeling of discovery. I've never known what real happiness was before.'

'Uh—'

'It'll take years to build up a coherent picture. What you can tell us will have to be correlated with the archeological evidence. No hurry, no need to rush you. Why not come to my place for dinner tonight? We'll relax, maybe have a few drinks and some music—'

'Uh . . . no. No, thanks. I'm busy.'

'Tomorrow, then? My wife would like to meet you. Father knows I've been talking of nothing else at home.'

'All right.' Langley felt like a skunk. When the interview was over, he had to restrain himself from saying good-by.

The sun slipped down under the horizon. Langley and Marin ate supper in the apartment without tasting it. Her eyes were thoughtful as they looked across a twilit world.

'Will you miss Earth?' he asked.

She smiled gently. 'A little. Now and then. But not too much, with you around.'

He got up and took a gown from the clothes chute for her. With its cowl over her hair, she had an appealing boyish look, a very youthful student. 'Let's go,' he said.

They went out the hall, to the flange and the moving bridgeway. A crowd laughed and chattered around them, gaily dressed, off on a restless hunt for pleasure. The lights were a hectic rainbow haze.

Langley tried to suppress the tension within himself. There was nothing to be gained by this jittering wonder about the forces leagued against him. Relax, breathe deep, savor the night air and the vision of stars and spires. Tomorrow you may be dead.

He couldn't. He hoped his wire-taut nerves weren't shown by his face. Walk slowly, gravely, as befits a man of learning. Forget that you have a gun under your arm.

The Twin Moons was a fairly well-known tavern of the slightly shady kind, nestled on the roof above low-level, just under the giant leap of metal which was Interplanetary Enterprises Tower. Walking in, Langley found himself in a Martian atmosphere, deep greenish-blue sky, a modern canal and an ancient fragment of red desert. There was a blur of scented smoke and the minor-key whine of a Martian folk song. Private booths were arranged along one wall with the appearance of caves in a tawny bluff; opposite was a bar and a stage, on which a shapely ecdysiast was going through her contortions in a bored fashion. The timeless hum and clatter of a well-filled inn was low under the music.

2045. Langley elbowed up to the bar. 'Two beers,' he said. The robot extended an arm with glasses, pumped them full from the arm itself, and sprouted a metallic hand for the money.

A man with the sun-darkened skin and gangling build of a Martian nodded at him. 'Don't see many professors in a place like this,' he remarked.

'It's our night out,' said Langley.

'Mine, too, I suppose. Can't wait to get home again, though. This planet's too heavy. 'Course, Mars is all shot these days, too. We ran the Solar System once. Those were the good old days. Now we're just nice obedient children of the Technon, like everybody else—'

A black uniform came up behind. The Martian snapped his mouth shut and tried to look innocent.

'Excuse me, sir,' said the policeman. He tapped Langley's shoulder. 'They're waiting for you.'

The spaceman's world buckled – just for a moment, then he recognized the now beardless face under the helmet. This man had pulled a blaster on Brannoch's agents, down in the slums. It seemed very long ago.

'Of course,' he said, and followed him. Marin trailed behind. They entered a booth.

It was full of uniforms. One bulky shape wore light combat armor; Valti's tones came through the helmet. 'Good evening, captain, my lady. Is everything clear?'

'Yes. All set, I think.'

'This way. I have an understanding with mine host.' Valti pressed his finger to a spot on the decorative design. The rear wall opened, and the first stairs Langley had seen in this age led upward to a tiny room where two uniforms of Ministerial military officers were laid out. 'Put them on, please,' said Valti. 'I think you can better act an aristocrat than a slave. But let me do the talking, except to Saris.'

'O.K.'

Marin shed her robe and climbed into the tunic with no sign of embarrassment. Hair drawn up under a light steel cap, cloak falling carelessly from her shoulders, she could pass for a teen-age Minister who had pulled rank to come along on this mission for a lark.

Valti explained the plan, then led the way down again, out the booth and into the street. The party numbered a score. It seemed very little to throw against all the might of Sol.

Nothing was said as the bridgeways carried them toward the military research center on the western edge of town. Langley wanted to hold Marin's hand, but that was impossible just now. He sat thinking his own thoughts.

Their destination was a tower jutting up from the sheer clifflike wall of the city; it stood somewhat apart from its neighbors, and there must be guns and armor behind its smooth plastic façade. As Valti's group got off onto a central flange and walked toward the entrance, three slave guards stepped from an offside niche. They bowed in unison, and one asked their business.

'Special and urgent,' said Valti. The box over his head muffled his accent. 'We are to remove a certain object of study secretly to a safer place. Here are our papers.'

One of the guards trundled out a table bearing instruments. The authorization was scanned microscopically; Langley guessed that Technon documents had some invisible code number which was changed daily at random. The retinal patterns of several men were scanned and compared with those recorded on the papers. Then the chief sentry nodded. 'Very good, sir. Do you require assistance?'

'Yes,' said Valti. 'Bring a police van around for us. We'll be out soon. And don't admit anyone else till we're gone.'

Langley thought of automatic guns hidden in the walls. But the door dilated for him and he followed Valti down a corridor. They went past several pillbox rooms whose personnel did not interfere, then had to stop at a second check point. After that they went on to Saris' prison; the papers told them where it was.

The Holatan lay on a couch behind bars. The rest of the chamber was an enigmatic jumble of laboratory equipment. There were sentries with mechanical as well as energy guns, and a pair of technicians working at a desk. They had to call up their boss for another discussion before they could release their captive.

Langley had gone up to the cell. Saris made no sign of recognition. 'Hello,' said the spaceman softly, in English. 'Are you all right?'

'Yess. So far they iss only electrical and other measurementss made. But iss hard to be caged.'

'Have you been taught the present language?'

'Yess. Very well, better than English.'

Langley felt weak with relief. His whole precarious plan had depended on this one assumption and on the amazing Holatan linguistic ability.

'I've come to get you out,' he said. 'But it'll take some doing; you'll have to coöperate and risk your neck.'

Bitterness edged the bass purr: 'My life? Iss all? That iss not much . . . now.'

'Marin knows the facts and what my scheme is. Now you'll have to be told. But it'll be the three of us against everybody else.' Swiftly, the man sketched out his knowledge and plans.

The golden eyes flared with a quick fierce light, and muscles bunched under the fur. But the voice said only: 'Iss well. We will try it thus,' in a careful tone of boredom and hopelessness.

Valti won his point with the supervisor. A long metal box with a few airholes was pushed in on an antigravity sled. Saris was prodded into it from his cell, and the lid locked over him. 'Shall we go, my lord?' asked Valti.

'Yes,' said the American. 'The arrangements are complete.'

Several men pushed the floating box back down the halls. Even with its weight nullified, the inertia was still considerable, and turning on the propulsion unit might set off automatic alarm. When they came back on the flange, a large black flier hovered waiting for them. Saris' crate was put into the rear compartment, the men piled in with it or into the cab, and Valti started it off for the Centaurian embassy.

Shoving back his helmet for a breath of air, the trader revealed a sweating face. 'This is getting more ticklish by the minute,' he complained. 'If only we could go direct to my flitter! That superintendent back in the lab will be calling up Chanthavar soon, I'll bet my nose, and then the grease will be off the griddle!'

Langley debated trying his scheme now, before they took on the next enemy. By-passing Brannoch entirely— No. There wasn't time. And Saris was almost helpless behind a mechanical lock. He bit his lip and waited.

The van stopped near the ambassadorial tower, of which the League had the upper third for apartments and offices. Valti led half his group toward the entrance. Again he had to produce papers and go through a check; Chanthavar was keeping the place heavily guarded. This time his ostensible orders were to remove certain key Centaurian personnel – he hinted that they were to be taken on a one-way ride, and the chief watchman grinned.

'Fetch the box in,' reminded Langley.

'What?' asked Valti, astonished. 'Why, my lord?'

'They may try something desperate. You never know. This will be a shock to them. Best to be prepared.'

'But will the . . . device . . . function properly, my lord?'

'It will. I've tested it.'

Valti teetered on the edge of decision, and Langley felt sweat start out on his palms. If the trader said no—!

'All right, my lord. It may be a good idea at that.'

The box wavered slowly through an opened portal. There was no one in sight, the lesser fry must be sleeping in their own quarters. Brannoch's private door was ahead. It opened as they approached, and the Thorian loomed huge in it.

'What's this?' he asked coldly. His heavy form crouched under the wildly colored pajamas, ready for a final despairing leap at their guns. 'I didn't invite you.'

Valti threw back his helmet. 'You may not be sorry for this call, my lord,' he said.

'Oh . . you. And Langley too, and – Come in!' The giant led them to his living room. 'What's this, now?'

Valti explained. The triumph flaring in his face made Brannoch look inhuman.

Langley stood by the floating metal coffin. He couldn't speak to Saris, couldn't warn him of anything or tell him, '*Now.*' The Holatan lay blind in an iron dark, only the senses and powers of his mind to reach forth.

'You hear that, Thrymka?' shouted Brannoch. 'Let's go! I'll call the men—'

'No!'

Brannoch checked himself in mid-stride. 'What's the matter?'

'Do not call them,' said the artificial voice. 'We have expected this. We know what to do. You go with them, alone; we will follow soon on our sled.'

'What in all space—'

'*Hurry!* There is more at stake than you know. Chanthavar may come any instant, and we have much to do yet.'

Brannoch wavered. Given a moment to think, he would remember Saris' abilities, notice the sudden slight accent of his Thrymans. But he had just been roused from sleep, he was used to obeying their orders –

Valti shoved him. Relief was obvious on the florid countenance. 'They're right, my lord. It'd be devilish hard to get their tank out inconspicuously, and take minutes to collect all your men. Let us be gone!'

Brannoch nodded, kicked his feet into a pair of shoes, and went out the door between his supposed guards. Langley stole a glance at Marin, her face was white with strain. He hoped the crazy thunder of his own heart didn't show.

So far, so good. Stopping at the embassy had been un-avoidable, but the extra opposition picked up there had been kept down to one man – and a man whom Langley's conscience required should be told the truth.

Saris had not only meant to take control of the Thryman microphones, but to short-out the circuits of their anti-gravity sled, leave them sitting helplessly behind. Had he done that – was he strong enough?

Perhaps!

It would be strange, though, if those shrewd and sus-picious intelligences were content with an arrangement which would leave them the prisoners of any accident. There must be means for repairing the apparatus, robot tools con-trollable from inside the tank. There were surely means of calling up the entire ring of Centaurian spies and saboteurs, throwing them all away just to break through Chanthavar's men and get into a concealed spaceship and flee.

The Thrymans were going to escape. There was no way of preventing that. They were probably going to pursue. And Chanthavar wouldn't be peacefully asleep much longer, either. The question was whether Valti's group could get out of tracer range before one or the other party was in action.

It'll be interesting to find out, thought Langley.

CHAPTER TWENTY

IN his own forgotten world, they would never have ac-complished this much. Somewhere along the line, there would have been a man with enough independence of mind to hold up the proceedings while he checked with his superiors. But a slave is not bred or trained to think for himself. This may be one reason why freedom, unstable, inefficient, stamped to oblivion again and again, still rises new through all history.

The van slipped swiftly across a darkened planet. Lora became a bright star cluster on the horizon, and then it was lost, only night could be seen. Langley doubted that he would ever look on that city again. It had flashed over his experience for a few weeks, but now it was as if it and all its millions had never been. It gave him some understanding of Valti's philosophy, his acceptance of the impermanent and the doomed as essential to the scheme of things.

Brannoch's sinewy face was etched against shadow by the dim light of the instrument panel. 'Do you know why the Society has decided to help us?' he asked.

'No, I don't, my lord,' said the trader.

'There's money in it somewhere. Big money. Unless you plan some treachery—' For a moment, teeth gleamed white, then the Thorian laughed. 'No. Why should you bother with me at all, if not for the purpose you stated?'

'Of course, my lord, the League will not be ungrateful for all my exertions?'

'Oh, yes, yes, you'll have your squeeze, never fear. I'll get it back from Earth. This does mean war, you know. There's no stopping the war now. But if I know these fat-gutted Ministers, they'll keep their fleet in this system to protect their own precious hides – long enough to give us a chance at the nullifier. We'll make a couple of heavy raids just to throw a scare into them.' Brannoch stared darkly ahead of him. 'I wonder what Thrymka wanted to stay for. I wonder how big their web really is. Some day I hope to do something about them too . . . the damned spiders!'

The van slanted toward a small clump of forest. When it grounded, Valti tumbled out. 'I've got the flitter here. If you please, sirs!'

A blaster cut the lock on Saris' box. The Holatan emerged

in one supple bound, and the party groped forward between trees.

'They iss all wit' energy weaponss here,' murmured the alien in English. 'All but one, the tall fellow there. Can you handle him?'

'I'd better be able to,' said Langley between clenched jaws.

The flitter loomed huge in the grove, like a pillar of night. 'Where are the rest of your gang?' asked Brannoch as he went up the ladder to the air lock.

'Snugly in bed, my lord,' said Valti. His voice sounded loud and flat in the immense hush. Somewhere, far off, crickets were chirping. It would probably be the last time he heard crickets, thought Langley. 'I'll have to get out of the Solar System, of course, but that's no reason to break up the rest of the organization.'

Twenty men to capture.

This spaceboat was meant for velocity rather than comfort. A single long room held passenger chairs and the pilot's seat. Valti sloughed off his armor, planted his large bottom in the control chair, and moved thick fingers in an astonishingly graceful dance over the panel. The boat shivered, roared, and leaped for the sky.

Atmosphere fell behind. Earth rolled huge and lovely against a curtain of incandescent stars. Langley looked at her with a wrenching of farewell.

Good-by, Earth. Good-by, hill and forest, tall mountains, windy plains, great march of seas under the moon. Good-by, Peggy.

A computer chattered quietly to itself. Lights blinked on the panel. Valti locked a switch in place, sighed gustily, and turned around. 'All right,' he said, 'she's on automatic, a high-acceleration path. We'll reach our ship in half an hour. You may as well relax.'

'Easier said than done,' grunted Brannoch.

It grew very still in the narrow metal chamber.

Langley threw a glance at Saris. The Holatan nodded, ever so faintly. Marin saw the gesture, and her own head bobbed. It was time.

Langley put his back to the wall near the controls. He drew his blaster. 'Don't move,' he said.

Someone cursed. A gun jumped up with blinding speed. It didn't fire.

'Saris has a grip on every weapon in here except mine and Marin's,' said Langley. 'You'd better sit still and listen— No, you don't!' He sent a beam roaring at the tall man with the old-style weapon. The trader howled as it fell from seared fingers.

'Sorry to do that.' Langley spoke low. There was sweat trickling down his face. 'I don't want to hurt anybody. But there are some pretty big issues involved. Will you give me a chance to explain?'

'Captain—' Valti shuffled closer. Marin waved him back with a ferocious gesture. Saris crouched in the after end of the room, shivering with effort.

'Listen to me.' Langley felt a vague annoyance that his tone should be pleading. Wasn't the man with the gun supposed to be unquestioned boss? But Valti's little eyes were shifting back and forth, watching for any chance at all. Brannoch's legs were gathered under his chair, ready to leap. The trader spacemen were snarling, building up courage for a rush to overwhelm him.

'I just want to tell you some facts,' said Langley. 'You've all been the dupes of one of the biggest, brassiest swindles in history. You think you're working for your own good – Valti, Brannoch – but I'm going to show you otherwise. You've got half an hour to wait in any event, so you might as well listen to me.'

'Go ahead,' said Brannoch thickly.

The American drew a shaky breath and launched into his account: the subversion of League and Technate and

Society by a foreign and hostile power working for its own ends. He gave Valti the spool he had along, and the man put it in a scanner and studied it with maddening deliberation. A clock spun off lazy minutes, and Earth receded in the boat's wake. The room was hot and silent.

Valti looked up. 'What are you going to do if I don't coöperate?' he asked.

'Make you.' Langley waved his gun.

The bushy red head shook, and there was a curious dignity over the pot-bellied form. 'No. I'm sorry, captain, but it won't go. You can't operate a modern spaceship, you don't know how, and my old carcass isn't worth so much that I'll do it for you.'

Brannoch said nothing, but his eyes were chips of blue stone.

'Can't you see, man?' shouted Langley. 'Can't you *think*?'

'Your evidence is very slender, captain. All the facts are susceptible of other interpretations.'

'When two hypotheses conflict, choose the simpler one,' said Marin unexpectedly.

Valti sat down. He rested his chin on one fist, closed his eyes, and looked suddenly old.

'You may be right,' said Brannoch. 'I've had my suspicions of those animated pancakes for a long time. But we'll deal with them later – after Thor is in a stronger position.'

'No!' cried Langley. 'You blind fool, can't you see? This whole war is being engineered by them. They must regard men as dangerous vermin. They can't conquer us by themselves, but they can get us to bleed each other white. Then *they* can mop up!'

A bell rang. Langley turned his head, and brought it around at Marin's scream. Brannoch was almost on him. He waved the Centaurian back, who grinned impudently, but let Valti go up to look at the instruments.

The trader faced them all and announced flatly: 'Someone has slapped a tracer beam on us. We're being followed.'

'Who? How far? How fast?' Brannoch snapped the questions out like an angry dog.

'I don't know. It may be your friends from Thrym, it may be Chanthavar.' Valti fiddled with some knobs and considered the readings of meters. 'Good-sized ship. Overhauling us, but we'll get to ours about ten minutes ahead of them. It takes a while to warm up the generators for an interstellar jump, so we may have to fight during that time.' His eyes were steady on Langley. 'If the good captain will permit that.'

The American drew a shuddering breath. 'No. I'll let them blow us all up first.'

Valti chuckled. 'Do you know, captain, I believe you. *And* your somewhat fantastic hypothesis.'

'That you'll have to prove,' said Langley.

'I shall. Men, please toss all your guns over here. The captain can mount guard on us if he won't find it boring.'

'Wait a minute—' A nomad stood up. 'Are you going against the orders of the chiefs?'

'I am – for the good of the Society.'

'I won't!'

Valti's answer cracked like a pistol shot. 'You will, sir, or I'll personally break your back across my knee. I'm your skipper this trip. Shall I read you the articles concerning obedience to the skipper?'

'I . . . yes, sir. But I'll file a complaint at—'

'Do so by all means,' agreed Valti cheerfully. 'I'll be right there in the office with you, filing my own.'

The blasters clattered at Langley's feet. Saris lay down, trembling with exhaustion.

'Tie up Brannoch,' said the American. 'In God we trust, but I don't think he's God.'

'Of course. You'll pardon the liberty, my lord? We'll leave you in the flitter, you can free yourself and scoot away.'

Brannoch glared murder, but submitted.

'Are you satisfied, captain?' asked Valti.

'Perhaps. Why do you believe me now?'

'Partly the evidence you showed, partly your own sincerity. I respect your intelligence.'

Langley shoved his blaster back into its sheath. 'O.K.!'

It had seemed a chancy thing to do, but Valti only nodded and resumed the pilot's chair. 'We've almost arrived,' he said. 'Time to put on the brakes and match velocities.'

The spaceship grew enormously. She was a long black cylinder, floating through a wilderness of stars. Langley saw her gun turrets stark against the Milky Way. There was a slight shock, a noise of metal making contact, and the boat had joined air locks.

'Battle stations!' snapped Valti. 'You may come with me, captain.' He plunged toward the exit.

Langley stopped by Brannoch. The giant met his eyes and gave him a savage grin. 'Good work,' he said.

'Look,' answered the spaceman, 'When you get loose, flit away from here but not too far. Listen in on any radio conversation. Think over what I've told you. Then, if you're wise, you'll get in touch with Chanthavar.'

'I . . . may.'

'God help you if you don't. Good-by, Brannoch.'

Langley went through the air lock. He was the last man, and the ship's outer door clashed to behind him. He didn't know the layout of this cruiser, but followed his hunches as he ran down the corridors. There was a roaring of machines about him, the ship was making ready to fight.

He located the main control chamber in a few minutes. Valti sat there, with Marin and Saris hovering in the background. The vessel must be almost entirely automatic, a robot in her own right, for one man to guide her thus.

A stellar globe gave a simulacrum of the cold star-spattered dark outside. Valti located a moving speck on it and adjusted a telescreen for an enlarged view. The approaching ship was a steel sphere.

'Thryman make,' said Valti. 'I'd know those lines anywhere. Let's see what they have to say.' He punched the radio keys.

Thryman! Then they must have escaped almost as soon as the others were gone, bulling through with the guns they doubtless had somewhere on their tank, reaching a hidden warship and taking it into space with nearly impossible speed. They would have known the orbit of Valti's craft from the Technon. Langley shivered, and Marin huddled close to him.

'Hello, Thrymka.' Valti spoke almost casually into his set. Eyes and hands were still moving, punching buttons, adjusting dials, observing the ready lights which flashed on for one compartment after another through his vessel.

The machine voice crackled back: 'You have been followed. If you are wise, you will surrender to us at once. The Solar patrols got a tracer on us, they are following close behind, and rather than let them have you, we will destroy everything.'

Solar! Langley whistled. Chanthavar had been pretty quick on the draw too, it seemed. But, of course, the Thryman getaway would have alerted him if nothing else did.

'Party's getting sort of crowded,' he muttered.

Valti threw down a switch. The celestial globe reflected tiny splotches of fire which must be earthshaking explosions.

'The ships fight themselves,' he remarked calmly. 'Our crew has little to do but stand by the emergency manual controls in case we take a hit.'

The two craft maneuvered for position, hurling their own tonnage through the sky as lightly as a fencer dances. Nuclear missiles flashed out, to be hunted down and exploded by counter-missiles. Long-range energy beams probed heaven with lightning. All that Langley sensed was the howl of generators, the crazy dance of sparks in the globe, and the busy clicking of the ship's robot brain.

Saris snarled hungrily. 'Could I be out there myself!' he raged. 'Could I get my teeth in them!'

Langley drew Marin to him. 'We may be rubbed out before we can break free,' he said. 'I feel awfully helpless.'

'You did wonderfully, Edwy,' she answered.

'Well . . . I tried. I love you, Marin.'

She sighed with a great happiness. 'That is enough.'

The walls trembled, and the air was filled with anger. A voice choked from the intercom: 'Near miss at Seven, sir. Outer plates holed, radiation blast, no air loss yet.'

'Carry on,' said Valti.

Even a nuclear explosion had to be very close to do much damage in vacuum. But a single shell which did touch the ship before going off would make molten rain of her.

'Here comes Chanthavar,' said Valti. 'I have an idea. He'll be listening in on the radio, so—' He flipped the keys. 'Hello, Thrymka. Hello, there. The Solarians are going to be on us in a minute. I like them even less than you, so let's settle our own differences later, shall we?'

There was no reply. The Thrymans never wasted speech, and they must see through such a transparent fraud.

But two Solar cruisers were sweeping in, and they had heard. The nearest turned in a graceful arc which would have been impossible without the gravity drive, and opened fire on the Thryman ship. Valti whooped and sent his vessel surging forward. One craft could not withstand the assault of two.

The screens did not show that eye-searing detonation. They refused the load, went blank, and when they functioned again a few seconds later the Thrymans were a rapidly expanding cloud of gas.

The two Solar warcraft circled cautiously, probing at the nomad with a few shells and beams. A siren hooted, Valti laughed aloud. 'The superdrive is ready. We can pull out of here now.'

'Wait,' said Langley. 'Call them up. I want to speak to them.'

'But they may fall on us together while we parley and—'

'Man, Earth has got to know too! Call them!'

But it was Chanthavar who came in first. His voice snapped crisply from the communicator: 'Hello, there, Society. Stand by to be boarded.'

'Not so fast, buster.' Langley leaned over Valti's shoulder, seeking the microphone. 'We can pull a switch and be ten light-years away, but I've got something to tell you.'

'Oh . . . you.' Chanthavar's tone held something close to amusement. 'You again! My respect for amateurs has gone up considerably tonight. I'd like to have you on my staff.'

'You won't. Now listen.' Langley rattled off what he knew as fast as he could.

There was a humming stillness. Then Chanthavar said slowly: 'Can you prove this?'

'You can prove it to yourself. Study the same documents I did. Pull in all the Centaurian agents you can find and question them – the Thrymans must have some humans in their pay. Put the facts and the hypothesis before the Technon, ask it for a re-evaluation. It must be capable of adding two and two!'

'You . . . may be right, Langley. You may be right.'

'You can bet I'm right. The Thrymans have no use for us. We're as monstrous to them as they are to us, and the war they had to fight convinced them we're dangerous to boot. Their aim must be nothing more or less than the extermination of the entire human race. Perhaps I'm wrong – but can you afford to take a chance on it?'

'No,' said Chanthavar quietly. 'It doesn't look that way.'

'Get hold of Brannoch. He's floating around somewhere in this vicinity. You and he and the Society – all the planets – are going to have to bury your little ambitions. If you don't, you're through. Together you can face anything.'

'We'll need that nullifier effect.'

'No, you won't. You can't conquer a planet the size of Thrym, but you can drive its natives back and keep them there if you all combine forces. Afterward, it'll be a healthy knowledge for you that somewhere in the galaxy is a planet of free men who have a weapon you can't stop. It may even give you some ideas about freeing yourselves.

'Good-by, Chanthavar. Good luck!'

He switched off the radio and stood up, feeling a sudden enormous calm. 'O.K.,' he said. 'Let's travel.'

Valti gave him a strange look; only later, remembering, did he recognize it as the look a man gives his leader. 'Best to go to Cygni first and let the Society – the *real* Society – know.'

'Yes,' agreed Langley. 'Then to Holat, to build defenses for them as we promised. You're going home, Saris.'

The great dark head rubbed against his knees.

'And then?' asked Valti. His hands were setting up the control pattern for the jump.

'And then,' said Langley with an exuberant laugh, 'Marin and I are off to find us a world where *we* can feel at home!'

'Do you mind if I come along?' whispered Valti.

Marin gripped Langley's hand. They regarded each other, without eyes for anything else. And when they looked around them again, there was a new sun in the sky.

THE END

Isaac Asimov, Grand Master of Science Fiction, in Panther Books

Panther Science Fiction — A Selection from the World's Best S.F. List

More Great Science Fiction Books from Panther

DOUBLE STAR	Robert A. Heinlein	35p	☐
BEYOND THIS HORIZON	Robert A. Heinlein	35p	☐
STRANGE RELATIONS	Philip José Farmer	35p	☐
THE LEFT HAND OF DARKNESS			
	Ursula K. LeGuin	35p	☐
CITY OF ILLUSIONS	Ursula K. LeGuin	35p	☐
THE LATHE OF HEAVEN	Ursula K. LeGuin	35p	☐
THE FREDERIK POHL OMNIBUS	Frederik Pohl	40p	☐
THE WONDER EFFECT			
	Frederik Pohl & C. M. Kornbluth	40p	☐

The Classic LENSMAN series
TRIPLANETARY	E. E. 'Doc' Smith	35p	☐
FIRST LENSMAN	E. E. 'Doc' Smith	40p	☐
GALACTIC PATROL	E. E. 'Doc' Smith	35p	☐
GREY LENSMAN	E. E. 'Doc' Smith	35p	☐
SECOND STAGE LENSMEN	E. E. 'Doc' Smith	35p	☐
CHILDREN OF THE LENS	E. E. 'Doc' Smith	40p	☐
MASTERS OF THE VORTEX	E. E. 'Doc' Smith	35p	☐

The Classic SKYLARK series
THE SKYLARK OF SPACE	E. E. 'Doc' Smith	40p	☐
SKYLARK THREE	E. E. 'Doc' Smith	40p	☐
SKYLARK OF VALERON	E. E. 'Doc' Smith	40p	☐
SKYLARK DUQUESNE	E. E. 'Doc' Smith	40p	☐
THE IRON DREAM	Norman Spinrad	40p	☐
SLAN	A. E. van Vogt	30p	☐
MOONBEAST	A. E. van Vogt	35p	☐

All these books are available at your local bookshop or newsagent; or can be ordered direct from the publisher. Just tick the titles you want and fill in the form below.

Name_____

Address_____

_____

Write to Panther Cash Sales, PO Box 11, Falmouth, Cornwall TR10 9EN
Please enclose remittance to the value of the cover price plus 15p postage and packing for one book plus 5p for each additional copy. Overseas customers please send 20p for first book and 10p for each additional book.
Granada Publishing reserve the right to show new retail prices on covers, which may differ from those previously advertised in the text or elsewhere.